# L.A. Confidential

The Screenplay

D1051959

# *L.A. CONFIDENTIAL*
# HAS THE CRITICS RAVING!

"Resplendently wicked, vastly entertaining . . . brilliantly adapted from James Ellroy's near-unfilmable cult novel."

—Janet Maslin, *New York Times*

"Hanson and Helgeland have taken a massively complex novel by James Ellroy and boiled it down to a no-flab screenplay."

—David Ansen, *Newsweek*

"Co-screenwriters Helgeland and Hanson have expertly extracted the essence of the proceedings and boiled them down to a concentrated screen story . . . a dark, dangerous, and intoxicating tale of big trouble in paradise."

—Kenneth Turan, *Los Angeles Times*

"It is amazing and gratifying to see the brilliant way that the book has been condensed into a labyrinthine yet never confusing narrative. . . . It's the best crime thriller since *Chinatown*."

—Rex Reed, *New York Observer*

"Hanson and Helgeland turn pulpmeister James Ellroy's brutal, bustling novel into something like cinematic gold."

—Richard Schickel, *Time*

# L.A. Confidential

The Screenplay
by

# Brian Helgeland
&
# Curtis Hanson
Based on the novel by
# James Ellroy

WARNER BOOKS

A Time Warner Company

Copyright © 1997 by Brian Helgeland & Curtis Hanson
Foreword © 1997 by Curtis Hanson
Foreword © 1997 by Brian Helgeland
Introduction © 1997 by James Ellroy
Photographs by Merrick Morton and Peter Sorel. Copyright © 1997 Monarchy Enterprises B. V. and Regency Entertainment (USA), Inc.

Veronica Lake from *This Gun For Hire,* courtesy of Universal Pictures. Copyright © 1942.

Warner Books, Inc., 1271 Avenue of the Americas, New York, NY 10020
Visit our Web site at
http://warnerbooks.com

 A Time Warner Company

Printed in the United States of America
First Printing: October 1997
10   9   8   7   6   5   4   3

ISBN: 0-446-67427-3
LC: 97-61469

*Book design by Stanley S. Drate/Folio Graphics Co. Inc.*
*Cover design by Diane Luger*
*Cover photography by Peter Sorel*

# Contents

# Foreword by
# Curtis Hanson

Naturally, it started with the book. I read James Ellroy's book for fun, as I had a half a dozen of his others. Many find Ellroy's novels unremittingly dark. I don't. His humor and strength of personality shine through. He's a survivor. Whether he intends it or not, that strength of spirit illuminates even the darkest of his nightmare visions.

With *L.A. Confidential* I got hooked on the characters, even though at first I didn't like them. Bud White seemed to be nothing more than a mindless thug; Ed Exley, an ambitious opportunist masquerading as an idealist; Jack Vincennes, a publicity hound exploiting the misery of others. But I got sucked in, emotionally involved in their battles with their personal demons. Sucked in by the discovery that while each character appears to be one thing when you meet them, the reality is something else (Lynn Bracken only *looks like* Veronica Lake). And all of them inhabit a city famous for creating illusions and manufactured images—Los Angeles, the city I grew up in, a city easy to dislike, but that I love.

I had to make the movie. I had to let these characters take me on my own journey to the Los Angeles of memory. But how to get a script from James Ellroy's labyrinthine novel, so intricately constructed with complex subplots, back stories and blind alleys?

Here's where luck entered the picture. I met Brian Helgeland, a screenwriter of (at that time) limited credits, but with a passion for *L.A. Confidential* and its characters that matched my own. We teamed up. Brian brought to the partnership his thoughtfulness, sense of humor, perseverance and enormous talent.

We went to work. We took many liberties with the plot, but we tried to be true to the ones who brought us—Ellroy's characters. If Bud, Ed or Jack wasn't involved in a scene, it went by the board. Some were too good to let go of: the shootout at the abandoned auto court in San Berdoo that begins the novel, for example. We took it, moved it and let two of our trio take part. What would Ellroy say of all this? After a point, who cared? We did. Without him, we wouldn't be there.

A word about James Ellroy. I was reluctant to meet him. Brian and I had our hands full with the book without getting involved with the man. Finally, when we had a draft with which we were comfortable, I called him. He was cordial, but wary. His attitude was, "My book, your movie." In other words, he'd take the money and hope for the best, but it was no skin off his nose one way or the other. I'm not sure I fully believed him, but I liked and respected him for saying it; this seems to me the only healthy attitude for a novelist to have.

We sent him the script anyway. His response was an invitation to meet him for dinner. The Pacific Dining Car, naturally. Brian and I had steaks and large drinks. Ellroy: shrimp, fish and lots of espresso. He liked the screenplay. More than liked it. He said we'd proven wrong his stated opinion that *L.A. Confidential* was the one book of his that would defy adaptation and never be made into a movie.

After Ellroy left, Brian and I stood talking by our cars for quite a while. We had formed a strong bond over many months working together, but now the partnership felt complete, blessed and joined by the man who had invented Bud White, Ed Exley and Jack Vincennes. There were high points yet to come—the picture being greenlit, actors cast—but nothing would match the pleasure and pride we felt that night in the parking lot of the Pacific Dining Car.

## Curtis Hanson
Los Angeles, California
June, 1997

# Foreword by
# Brian Helgeland

I first met James Ellroy in 1988. I watched him, studied him for about twenty minutes before I introduced myself. You see, I was standing in line inside a Hollywood Boulevard bookstore waiting for him to sign a hardcover edition of *The Big Nowhere*. I had just received my first screen credit a few months earlier, but I had come here to see what a "real writer" looked like. On the title page Ellroy scribbled, "To Brian—L.A. 1950 makes you do the Bad Boogaloo! James Ellroy." I went home. I had seen a real writer and, well, he didn't look at all like me. Little did I imagine that 1953 would be my year and that the novel would be *L.A. Confidential.*

When I heard the rights had been secured by Warner Bros., I began a year-long quest simply to get a meeting to pitch how I would adapt it given the chance. Finally, after much sweat and blood on my agent Missy Malkin's part, a meeting was set. I would have my day in court. Then, disaster. The meeting was canceled. I was informed that Curtis Hanson had been hired to write and direct the film. Thus began my second quest—to meet Curtis and convince him that I should be part of his ambitions.

We met in an old bungalow on the Universal lot that had been pink slipped—scheduled to be torn down to make way for the Jurassic Park portion of the studio tour. I thought this was a good sign, as much of the L.A. we would need to bring to life had suffered a similar fate. What quickly became clear was that we both shared a passion for the novel. Curtis was gracious enough to bring me aboard, and three years and a good ten drafts later, the film became a reality.

The scholars among you can read the novel and compare it to the screenplay. Hopefully you'll agree with and understand the choices we made. The bottom line, the guiding precept, was always to stay true to the characters. Exley, White, and Vincennes. Magnificent bastards all. In helping them to the screen, I felt like a guardian of the novelist's intent. For more than anything, I hope that we have done James Ellroy the "absolute justice" that his extraordinary characters and novel deserve.

Brian Helgeland
Malibu, California
June, 1997

# Introduction by
# James Ellroy

I wrote the novel *L.A. Confidential* in 1988 and '89. It was conceived and executed as the centerpiece of my *L.A. Quartet*—an epic pop history of my smogbound fatherland between the years 1947 and 1959. The first two volumes of the *Quartet*—*The Black Dahlia* and *The Big Nowhere*—dealt specifically with a hellish sex-killing and its ramifications, and the anticommunist hysteria that swept Hollywood in the early '50s. I wanted volume three to span eight full years and stand as an elegy to a big, expanding city on the make. My essential design was to cram real-life events and established historical characters into a series of complexly structured storylines, add fictional protagonists and antagonists, and rebuild and rewrite my hometown and my first formative decade to my own specifications.

I diagrammed the book in minute detail. The formal outline ran 250 pages. Eight inextricably linked plotlines formed the basic narrative. Three cop antiheroes bebopped with a supporting cast of characters that ran close to the three-digit mark. Fictional events transpired concurrent with my chronologically altered renditions of the "Bloody Christmas" police-brutality scandal, the building of the Southern California freeway system, the heyday of scandal-rag journalism, Mickey Cohen's inept reign as a mob kingpin, and the creation of a theme park disingenuously disguised to remind readers of Disneyland. I conceived and wrote *L.A. Confidential* on a grand scale. I recognized it as a work of jumbo revisionism and an exercise in benign megalomania.

I figured some movie-biz fuckhead would option the book. I figured he'd blow smoke up my ass about what a great film it would make. Movieland self-delusion was a major theme of the novel. It was only fitting that I should profit from its exercise. I knew my book was movie-adaptation-proof. The motherfucker was uncompressable, uncontainable, and unequivocally bereft of sympathetic characters. It was unsavory, unapologetically dark, untamable, and altogether untranslatable to the screen.

My rationale was ironclad. It turned out to be speciously reasoned and empirically unsound. I'm writing this introduction from the standpoint of joyous apostasy. Some gifted people came along and proved me wrong.

I'm from L.A. I'm obsessed with the L.A. before my birth and the L.A. of my youthful cognizance. My birthplace mandated the intellectual curiosity that fuels my obsession. If I was from Moosefart, Montana, or Dogdick, Delaware, I'd be obsessed with crime in those burgs. The dynamic is just that easily defined.

If you grew up in L.A. and grew up obsessed with crime, you would probably dig crime movies and very possibly recognize the existence of a showbiz/true crime/scandal rag matrix. Your imagination might get corrupted very young.

Mine did. I saw *Plunder Road* at age nine and learned that all daring heists go bad—because daring heist men are psychologically fucked-up and unconsciously self-destructive. I saw *Vertigo* several months later. James Stewart's descent into degradation for Kim Novak titillated and repulsed me. I cannot separate the film from a real-life event that followed it within a few weeks. My mother was murdered in a dusty town fourteen miles east of L.A. proper.

I knew that Rock Hudson was a homosexual before I hit puberty. My father subscribed to scandal rags and let me read them. I got the scoop on Ava Gardner's nympho status and Johnny Stompanato's size. Scandal sheets gave me an alternative reality to juxtapose against the crime movies I saw. I knew that most movies were manufactured dreams to sedate mass audiences and a few movies were nightmares made to thrill and scare the chosen few. The scandal rags—*Confidential, Lowdown, Rave, Whisper*—served as a concordance. They hipped the elite to the sex and moral confusion behind the beautiful faces seen on the screen. They vulgarized and eroticized and defined gods and goddesses as frail and attainable—for those with properly corrupted imaginations.

My passion for movies does not extend beyond their depiction of crime. My filmic pantheon rarely goes past 1959 and the end of the film noir age. My curiosity about the manufacture of films and journalistic sleazemongering remains fixed in that era. The era shaped and warped my perspective.

America was pre-psychologized. L.A. was pre-psychologized and hopped up on its own good looks and potential. Its vocabulary was all boosterism and innu-endo. The power of sex was magnified and rendered taboo by the absence of sustained dialogue. Everything forbidden and bad that is happening today was happen-ing then—in a much less high-tech manner and to a much lesser statistical degree. Relative safety spawned complacency and a covert sense of horror. It created a drama-enhancing balance that manifested itself in a dual-L.A. fashion. The outer L.A. was the placid world of movies as manufactured dreams. The secret L.A. was movies as nightmares—movies blurred by the glare of scandal-rag flashbulbs, movies that saw the manufac-ture of movies as a dark and corrupting endeavor.

I figured some people knew what I knew. I figured a few filmmakers did, too. I figured that *L.A. Confidential* would seduce them with its power and baffle them with its density and scope.

I was wrong again.

Curtis Hanson is an L.A. homeboy. He's fifty-two to my forty-nine. That slight age gap telescopes back to the '50s. He recalls the decade much better than I do.

We both grew up jazzed by crime. Hanson read Caryl Chessman's autobiography years before I did. We both had a red-hot jones for the Finch-Tregoff snuff of 1959.

We grew up on opposite sides of the Hollywood Hills. I became an L.A.-crime obsessed novelist. He became an L.A.-crime obsessed screenwriter and director. His road back to '50s L.A. was more circuitous than mine.

I was monomaniacally stuck in that time. Hanson

wasn't. He wrote and directed comedies, animal stories, romantic thrillers, and adventure films. I think he was waiting to take an epic fall for L.A. way back when.

I am not sufficiently egotistical to contend that all of the previous films that Curtis Hanson has written and directed are nothing but the road to *L.A. Confidential.* Hanson himself has called *L.A. Confidential* his best and most personal film—and I have no doubt that his future work will eclipse it. I also contend that *L.A. Confidential* will stand as his most challenging book-to-film adaptation.

What amazes me is that my book sparked a gifted and receptive co-scenarist/director, and the gifted and receptive co-scenarist Brian Helgeland, in a manner that inspired this screenplay and a spellbinding film. Curtis Hanson and I can point to our longstanding fixation with Los Angeles and say, "That's how I got here." Brian Helgeland—a Massachusetts transplant to L.A.—can't cop that plea.

Helgeland got hooked on the book and became a time-traveler. He immersed himself in the place and the era and brought a fresh intellect to the task of seeing, selecting, containing, compressing, and emphasizing the dramatic elements necessary to twist *L.A. Confidential* into a cohesive film form. I did not observe Helgeland and Hanson as they worked on this screenplay. I was not privy to their hundreds of hours of discussion and writing dialogue—separately and together. I can only say that they conquered my uncontrollable, uncontainable, uncompressable, unapologetically dark and unadaptable novel.

Critics often call my books "visual." Readers take my

black type on white paper and create subjective images that I will never see. This screenplay is the blueprint for a definitive visual version of *L.A. Confidential*—the novel as film. The film thrills me and moves me and troubles me. It's my world on celluloid—and a distinctly different, compatible world that I never could have imagined.

James Ellroy
Kansas City
May 31, 1997

# L.A. Confidential

The Screenplay

FADE IN:

*Over the opening strains of Johnny Mercer's "AC-CENT-TCHU-ATE THE POSITIVE," a MONTAGE: a mixture of headlines, newsreel footage and live action.* Economy Booming! Postwar Optimism! L.A.: City of the Future!

> HUDGENS' VOICE
> Come to Los Angeles. The sun shines bright. The beaches are wide and inviting and the orange groves stretch as far as the eye can see. There are jobs aplenty and land is cheap. Every working man can have his own house. And, inside every house—a happy all-American family. You can have all this. And, who knows? You could even be discovered. Become a movie star. Or at least see one. Life is good in Los Angeles. It's paradise on earth.

*We see images of everything Hudgens mentions: beaches, orange groves, assembly lines, tract housing, movie stars. Hudgens chuckles, his voice becomes more "confidential":*

> HUDGENS' VOICE
> That's what they tell you anyway. Because they're selling an image. They're selling it through movies, radio and television.

EXT. STORE FRONT – NIGHT

*A dozen people watch a display window TELEVISION*

*as it rolls the opening of the hit show* Badge of Honor. *A shot of City Hall and a make-believe homicide detective played by actor BRETT CHASE.*

> HUDGENS' VOICE
> In the hit show *Badge of Honor,* the L.A. cops
> walk on water as they keep the city clean of
> crooks. Yup, you'd think this place was the
> Garden of Eden. But there's trouble in paradise.

*A prominent headline in the montage:* GANGLAND! *Police photographers document crime scenes. The meat wagon hauls ex-button men to the morgue. Where will it end?*

> HUDGENS' VOICE
> And his name is Meyer Harris Cohen . . .

INT. THE MOCAMBO – NIGHT

*A CLUB PHOTOGRAPHER pops snapshots, but the real action is on the floor where MICKEY COHEN dances with two different GIRLS at once. A fireplug of a man, he hardly seems a public menace.*

> HUDGENS' VOICE
> Mickey C to his fans, local L.A. color to the nth
> degree. And his #1 bodyguard, Johnny
> Stompanato.

*Nearby is his bodyguard, JOHNNY STOMPANATO, his hair in a slick pompadour. A bottle of champagne pops; Stompanato reacts, nearly draws a pistol from his shoulder holster. As he laughs at himself . . .*

                    HUDGENS' VOICE
          Mickey C's the head of organized crime in these
          parts. He runs dope, rackets and prostitution.
          He kills a dozen people a year. And the dapper
          little gent does it in style.

*More headlines, shots of citizens engaged in illegal gambling, prostitution, and shots of Mickey.*

                    HUDGENS' VOICE
          And every time his picture's plastered on the
          front page, it's a black eye for the image of Los
          Angeles, because how can organized crime exist
          in the city with the best police force in the
          world? Something has to be done. But nothing
          too original. 'Cause, hey, this is Hollywood.
          What worked for Al Capone would work for the
          Mickster.

EXT. COHEN MANSION (BEVERLY HILLS) – DAY

*In monogrammed silk pajamas, Mickey Cohen answers the door, his pet BULLDOG Mickey Jr. at his feet. The police are waiting. REPORTERS' flashbulbs pop.*

POLICE OFFICER
Mr. Cohen, you're under arrest.


MICKEY COHEN
Bullshit. What's the charge?


POLICE OFFICER
Nonpayment of federal income tax.


MICKEY COHEN
*Bullshit.*


INT. *HUSH-HUSH* MAGAZINE OFFICE (SUNSET BLVD.) – NIGHT

*Lurid page-one headlines cover the wall where SID HUDGENS types. Hudgens is the publisher-photographer-writer of* Hush-Hush *magazine and keeper of inside dirt supreme. As he continues . . .*


HUDGENS
But all is not well. Sending Mickey up has created a vacuum. And it's only a matter of time before someone with balls of brass tries to fill it. Remember, dear readers, you heard it here first, off the record, on the QT and very *Hush-Hush.*


*The song ends and so does the montage.*

INT. PACKARD – 1486 EVERGREEN (SUBURBIA) –
NIGHT

*Behind the wheel, Wendell "BUD" WHITE, 32. An LAPD
cop, Bud's rep as the toughest man on the force has been
well-earned. Bud stares intently at a stucco house in a
row of vet prefabs. A neon SANTA SLEIGH has landed
on the roof. Through the front window, a BEEFY GUY
browbeats his WIFE. Puff-faced, 35-ish, she backs away
as he rages at her.*

*In the Packard's backseat, with cases of Walker Black
and Cutty Sark, is Bud's partner—DICK STENSLAND.*

*Older, but still tough despite his beer gut, "Stens" sucks on a pint of Old Crow. Stens sighs as Bud flips through a handwritten pad of names, addresses and dates.*

> STENSLAND
> You're like Santa Claus with that list, Bud. Except everyone on it's been naughty.

> BUD
> Here it is. Guy's been out on parole two weeks.

> STENSLAND
> Leave it for later. We got to pick up the rest of the booze and get it to the station.

*Bud picks up the radio.*

> BUD
> Hollywood, this is 6A-7. Have Central send a prowler to 1486 Evergreen. Male Caucasian Ralph Kinnard in custody. Aggravated assault, resisting arrest and assaulting a police officer. We won't be here, but they'll see him.

EXT. 1486 EVERGREEN – NIGHT

*Bud steps to the house.*

*Inside we hear slaps, muffled cries. Bud grips an outlet cord coming off the roof and yanks. The sleigh crashes to the ground with reindeer exploding around it. A beat. The Beefy Guy runs out to investigate, spots Bud.*

BEEFY GUY
Who the fuck are you?

BUD
The Ghost of Christmas Past. How'd you like to dance with a man for a change?

*The Beefy Guy takes a swing, misses. Bud digs a fist into his gut. Grabbing Beefy's hair, Bud drives his face to the pavement.*

BUD
Touch her again and I'll know about it. Understand? Huh?

*Another face full of cement. The Wife watches with apprehension from the steps as Bud cuffs her husband to a porch support.*

BUD
You'll be out in a year. You touch her again and I'm gonna get you violated on a kiddie raper beef. You know what they do to kiddie rapers up in Quentin? Huh?

*Bud empties Beefy's pockets. A cash roll and car keys. Bud looks over at the battered wife.*

                        BUD
You got someplace you can go?

*She nods. Bud hands her the keys and the cash.*

                        BUD
Go get yourself fixed up.

                        WIFE
                 *(nods; determined)*
Merry Christmas, huh?

*Bud watches as she gets into a prewar Ford in the drive.
She backs over a blinking reindeer as she goes.*

                     STENSLAND
Let's go, Bud. The boys will be waiting.


INT. VARIETY INTERNATIONAL PICTURES –
STAGE 4 – NIGHT

*The* Badge of Honor *set. A Christmas party in full swing.
Eating, drinking and dancing. Star BRETT CHASE, seen
earlier on television, is holding court.*

*Out on the dance floor, we meet the City of Angels' free-
wheeling, big time "Big V," celebrity crime stopper Sgt.
JACK VINCENNES, 38.*

*Possessed of slick good looks and a snappy wardrobe,
Jack dances with a young ACTRESS. Grinding their way*

*through "Oh! Look At Me Now," they're obviously hitting it off.*

ACTRESS
What exactly do you do on the show, Jack?

JACK
Technical advisor. I teach Brett Chase how to walk and talk like a cop.

*The Actress looks over, watches Chase a beat. She looks back at Jack, smiles.*

ACTRESS
Brett Chase doesn't walk and talk like you.

JACK
Television version. America isn't ready for the real me.

ACTRESS
Is it true you're the one who arrested Bob Mitchum?
(grinds closer)
These *Badge of Honor* guys like to pretend, but being the real thing must be a thrill.

JACK
Let's go someplace quiet. I'll give you the lowdown on Mitchum.

ACTRESS
You got your handcuffs with you?

JACK
Two sets.

ACTRESS
I'll get my coat.

*They're interrupted by Sid Hudgens.*

HUDGENS
Big V Jack Vincennes! May I have this dance?

JACK
Karen, this is Sid Hudgens from *Hush-Hush*
magazine.

HUDGENS
Helloooo, Karen.

ACTRESS
Hello, yourself.

*The Actress storms off. Jack looks to Sid for explanation.*

HUDGENS
We did a piece last year. "Ingenue Dykes in
Hollywood." Her name got mentioned.

JACK

Is it true?


HUDGENS

"Just the facts, ma'am." Look, Jackie-Boy, a friend of mine just sold some reefer to Matt Reynolds. He's tripping the light fantastic with Tammy Jordan at 2245 Maravilla, just up from the El Cortez.


JACK

You lost me, Sid. Who?

                    HUDGENS
Contract players at Metro. You pinch 'em. I do
you up feature in the next issue. Plus the usual
fifty cash.

                     JACK
I need an extra fifty. Two patrolmen at twenty
apiece and a dime for the watch commander at
Hollywood Station.

                    HUDGENS
Jack! It's Christmas!

                     JACK
No. It's felony possession of marijuana.

                    HUDGENS
Actually, it's circulation thirty-six thousand
and climbing.

*Jack starts out with Sid following.*

                    HUDGENS
No telling where this is gonna go, Jackie-Boy.
Radio, television. You whet the public's
appetite for the truth and the sky's the limit.


INT. HOLLYWOOD STATION – DISPATCH DESK –
NIGHT

*SGT. ED EXLEY, 30, stands with an* L.A. Herald Express
*REPORTER and PHOTOGRAPHER. They listen with*

*other COPS as a police captain (DUDLEY SMITH) sings "Silver Bells."*

*Exley is an up-and-comer. A police department poster boy. Burning with ambition. The faster he rises through the ranks, the more resentment he leaves in his wake.*

                    REPORTER
Sergeant Ed Exley, the son of the legendary
Preston Exley. Must be a hard act to follow?

*The Photographer snaps a picture.*

                    REPORTER
Why not make a mark somewhere else? Why
become a cop, Ed?

*Exley answers with a politician's smile.*

                    EXLEY
I like to help people.

                    REPORTER
We heard two officers were assaulted this
evening. What do you think about that?

                    EXLEY
It goes with the job. But I took the report.
Luckily they're okay.

PHOTOGRAPHER
Not what we heard.


REPORTER
Aren't you a little young to be watch
commander?


EXLEY
It's just for tonight. The married men have
Christmas Eve off.


REPORTER
That's a good lead for the story.

*They turn as Dudley finishes to applause. Fifty, hand-
some in his police captain's uniform, Dudley is tough,
respected, a department power to be reckoned with. As
he comes over:*


REPORTER
Captain Smith, I—


DUDLEY
Drop the formalities; it's Christmas Eve. Call
me Dudley.


REPORTER
Dudley, I came up with a title for the story. I'm
calling it "Silent Night with the LAPD."

                    DUDLEY
Excellent. How's this?
                  *(dramatic pause)*
The sanctity of the night is an invitation to the
darker criminal element. Our vigilance will not
be diminished.

*As the Reporter scribbles down the quote . . .*


                    DUDLEY
Remember, that's Smith with an S.

*The Reporters laugh. Dudley looks to Exley. They need
to talk.*


INT. HOLLYWOOD STATION – STAIR LANDING –
NIGHT

*TWO COPS walk down a passageway. One carries a tray
of glasses, the other, a sloshing bowl of EGGNOG.*


                    COP ONE
You hear about Brown and Helenowski? They
were off-duty. Got the shit kicked out of them
at some bar.

*At the foot of the stairs, they encounter Dudley and
Exley. As the Cops continue around them:*


                    DUDLEY
Hang on, lads.

*Dudley grabs two glasses, dips them into the nog. As the Cops go up the stairs, Dudley hands a glass to Exley.*

DUDLEY
*(a toast)*
To the memory of your father.

*They drink. Exley invokes his father's favorite toast:*

                    EXLEY
"To the solving of crimes that require absolute
justice."

*Exley raises his glass, but Dudley just watches him.*


                    DUDLEY
That was his favorite toast.
                    *(a beat)*
I saw the test results on the lieutenant's exam.
You placed first out of twenty-three.


                    EXLEY
The youngest applicant by eight years.


                    DUDLEY
You'll make lieutenant inside a year. Patrol
division? Internal Affairs?


                    EXLEY
I was thinking Detective Bureau.

*Dudley doesn't approve. He waits as a few more cops
make their way down the stairs and into the muster
room.*


                    DUDLEY
You don't have the eye for human weakness to

be a good detective. Or the stomach. You're a
political animal, Edmund.

*The criticism stings, but Dudley's a straight shooter.*

                    EXLEY
You're wrong.


                    DUDLEY
Am I? Would you be willing to plant
corroborative evidence on a suspect you knew
was guilty in order to ensure an indictment?


                    EXLEY
Dudley, we've been over this.


                    DUDLEY
Yes or no, Edmund.


                    EXLEY
I . . . no.


                    DUDLEY
Would you be willing to beat confessions out of
suspects you knew to be guilty?


                    EXLEY
No.

                    DUDLEY

Would you be willing to shoot hardened
criminals in the back to offset the chance—


                    EXLEY

*No.*


                    DUDLEY

Then for God's sake, don't be a detective. Stick
to assignments where you won't have to make
those choices. Patrol, Internal Affairs, but not
the Bureau.


                    EXLEY

I know you mean well, Dudley, but I don't need
to do it the way you did. Or my father.


                    DUDLEY

We'll see. Well, I've got to escort the press
downtown to the Chief's office.
                *(a beat)*
At least get rid of the glasses. I can't think of
one Bureau man who wears them.


*As Dudley goes back inside, Exley adjusts his glasses.*


EXT. NICK'S LIQUOR (HOLLYWOOD
NEIGHBORHOOD) – NIGHT

*The street crisscrossed with garish Christmas decora-*

*tions. It almost looks festive as Bud White's Packard pulls up.*


INT. NICK'S LIQUOR – NIGHT

*Tinsel-trimmed photos of movie stars look down from the walls as the OWNER loads a case of liquor for Bud, who waits across the counter. The Owner grumbles to himself, obviously supplying the stuff for free.*


> OWNER
> I ever get held up, you guys better be here.

*Bud looks across as LYNN BRACKEN enters. Her hair kerchiefed, there's glamour, a cat-girl grace about Lynn. Like she belongs up on the wall with the movie stars.*


> LYNN
> Nick, I need a delivery. A case each of gin, Scotch, and rum.


> OWNER
> *(manages a smile)*
> Sounds like a helluva party, Lynn. I'll be right with you.

*As the Owner continues loading the box, Lynn looks across at Bud. Bud doesn't look so tough for a moment. He says the only thing he can think of:*

                        BUD
Merry Christmas.


                        LYNN
Merry Christmas yourself, *Officer*.


                        BUD
That obvious, huh?


                        LYNN
                  *(smiles sweetly)*
It's practically stamped on your forehead.


*As the Owner bangs the case of liquor on the counter . . .*


EXT. NICK'S LIQUOR – NIGHT

*Bud exits with his booze, heads for the car and the waiting Stensland. Something catches his eye. A LINCOLN CONTINENTAL in the driveway up ahead blocking the sidewalk. A beautiful redhead is in the rear passenger seat. SUSAN LEFFERTS. Both her eyes are black, and her nose is bandaged.*

*Bud sets the case down on the car, starts over. Bud raps on Susan's window with his badge, motions for her to roll it down. The driver's side door opens and bodyguard LELAND "BUZZ" MEEKS menaces his way out.*

MEEKS

Get lost why don't you?

*As Meeks comes around the car, Bud grabs him, spins him around, forces him over the hood. He pats him down, finds a .38 in a shoulder holster.*

MEEKS

I got a license for that.

*Bud removes Meeks' wallet, checks the ID.*

MEEKS

Cut me some slack. I used to be a cop.

BUD

Leland Meeks? I never heard of you.

MEEKS

They call me Buzz.

BUD

I don't give a rat's ass what they call you. Now stay there, Buzz . . .

*Bud steps back to Susan's window.*

BUD

You okay?

*From beside her, a man in black tie leans over. PIERCE PATCHETT is a man used to being chauffeured. Like FDR, he smokes his cigarette in a holder.*

PATCHETT

She's fine.

BUD

I'm not asking you, sir.

*Something in Bud's tone tells Patchett he's walking on thin ice. Bud looks back to Susan.*

BUD

Somebody hit you?

LYNN
*(from behind)*
It's not what you think.

*Bud turns to see Lynn Bracken approaching from the liquor store.*

BUD

What is it then?

SUSAN
You got the wrong idea, Mister. I'm fine.

*Susan LAUGHS. Patchett eases back into the shadows.*

LYNN

But it's nice to know you care.

*Dismissing him, she gets in the car. Bud empties the .38 of shells, then hands it and the wallet back to Meeks.*

*As Meeks gets back in the car, Stensland steps up. The Lincoln starts to pull way.*

STENSLAND

What's going on?

*For an odd moment, Stensland and Meeks lock eyes through the windshield.*

BUD

You know him?

STENSLAND

Seen him around. He used to be a cop.

*Stensland laughs, picks up the case of booze.*

EXT. 2245 MARAVILLA (HOLLYWOOD) – NIGHT

*Just off the Boulevard with a view of the El Cortez. A klieg-lighted, limousine premiere is going on: WHEN WORLDS COLLIDE. Jack and two uniformed PATROL-MEN wait on the street. Hudgens' assistant, CHIP, holds*

*a portable arc light. Hudgens creeps back over from the
house.*

                    HUDGENS
    They're sitting in the dark, goofing on the
    Christmas tree.


                    JACK
              *(points to a spot)*
    You be there with your camera. I'll stop here so
    you get the movie premiere in the background.


                    HUDGENS
    I like it! "The Movie Premiere Pot Bust."


                    JACK
    And, Sid, when I bring them out the door, I do
    not want that goddamned baby spot of yours in
    my eyes.


                    HUDGENS
    Hear that, Chip? Consider it done, Jackie-Boy.


INT. 2245 MARAVILLA – NIGHT

*Jack peers through the glass in the front door. The scene
is romantic, almost sweet. Dino's singing on the hi-fi.*

*Two gorgeous kids (MATT REYNOLDS and TAMMY JOR-*
*DAN) necking in their BVDs by the glow of the Christmas*
*tree. Suddenly, the arc light floods the living room,*
*bleaching it white hot, and Jack kicks the door in. The*
*room is caught flush: the terrified kids, a bag of weed on*
*the couch between them.*

                              JACK
     Police!

EXT. 2245 MARAVILLA – NIGHT

*Jack exits, hauling Jordan and Reynolds by the neck, the blinding light in their faces. Sid bangs off photos. Jack stops with the movie premiere framed behind him and Hudgens clicks off a last shot.*

                    HUDGENS
        Got it! Cut! Wrap it!

*Windows light up. Rubberneckers appear. Jack hands the kids to the Patrolmen and heads back to the apartment. Hudgens hands Chip the camera.*

                    HUDGENS
        Chip! Get this in the soup!

INT. 2245 MARAVILLA – NIGHT

*Jack scoops the pot, flips through an address book. A card falls out. "Fleur-de-Lis. Whatever you desire . . ." Jack looks from the card out the window at the kids being loaded into a Black & White. They're both crying now. Hudgens comes in the door.*

                    HUDGENS
                  *(stentorian tone)*
        "It's Christmas morning in the City of Angels,
        and while decent citizens sleep the sleep of the
        righteous, hopheads prowl for marijuana, not

knowing that a man is coming to stop them. The freewheeling big-time Big V, celebrity crime-stopper Jack Vincennes, the scourge of grass-hoppers and junk fiends everywhere." You like it, Jackie-Boy?

JACK

Yeah, it's subtle.

*Sid hands him a President Grant 50.*

HUDGENS

"Remember, dear readers, you heard it here first, off the record, on the QT and very *Hush-Hush*."

EXT. HOLLYWOOD STATION – SIDE ENTRANCE – NIGHT

*Bud's Packard is parked by a door through which Bud and Stensland hustle cases of liquor. Stensland hands a case to a COP waiting in the doorway.*

COP

What took you guys?

STENSLAND

My partner stopped to make an arrest. His priorities are all screwed up.

*They laugh. Bud doesn't.*

INT. HOLLYWOOD STATION – DISPATCH DESK – NIGHT

*Exley's at the desk shuffling paper.*

*The big double doors open and Jack arrives followed by the two Patrolmen with Matt Reynolds and Tammy Jordan in tow. Jack, who regularly works out of the detective bureau at City Hall, is practically a movie star to the station house cops. They greet him with "Hey, Jack!," "Big V!," "To what do we owe this honor?!"*

> JACK
> Just keeping the streets safe, boys!
> *(to Patrolmen)*
> Book them.

*As the Patrolmen hustle the kids off, Jack steps over to Exley, drops a ten-dollar bill on the desk.*

> EXLEY
> What's that for, Vincennes?

> JACK
> You're watch commander tonight, aren't you?

> EXLEY
> Yeah. So?

JACK

A gratuity from *Hush-Hush* magazine. Get
yourself a new pair of loafers.

*Exley pushes the ten back to the edge of the desk.*


EXLEY

Keep your payoff. I'm not interested.

*Jack's about to respond when turmoil pushes in through
the double doors. Six handcuffed MEXICAN SUSPECTS
hustled in by a DOZEN COPS. Everyone shouting and
shoving. Exley steps forward, intercepts a YOUNG OF-
FICER.*


EXLEY

What the hell's this?


YOUNG OFFICER

Six spics, er, Mexicans, sir. The ones who
assaulted Brown and Helenowski.


JACK

I heard Helenowski lost six pints of blood. And
Brown's in a coma.


EXLEY

I took the report. They're home with bruises
and muscle pulls. Let's get these men booked
and into the lockup.

*No one listens. As word of the arrival of the suspects spreads . . .*

INT. SQUAD ROOM (HOLLYWOOD STATION) – NIGHT

*All alone, Bud types his report with one finger. Dogged, he gets the job done.*

INT. UPSTAIRS MUSTER ROOM (HOLLYWOOD STATION) – NIGHT

*An impromptu bar has been set up. The party is in full swing, the floor packed with NIGHTWATCH BLUES. A phonograph spews dirty Christmas carols. The liquor is flowing. Stensland, half in the bag, pours Old Crow into the water cooler. The cops around him talk.*

> INTOXICATED COP
> Hear what those taco benders did to Helenowski and Brown? Helenowski lost an eye, and they're reading Brown his last rites.

> STENSLAND
> We ought to teach Paco and his friends a lesson.

*More cops voice their agreement. Bottles are passed.*

INT. DISPATCH DESK (HOLLYWOOD STATION) – NIGHT

*The Mexicans are escorted through the door toward the*

*lockup. A group of cops moves to follow. Exley gets in front of them.*

> EXLEY
>
> All right, men. Back to work.

*But Exley's having trouble holding them back. There's fear in his eyes; the situation's threatening to get out of control.*

*Coming down the stairs from the muster room, Stensland finds himself eye to eye with Exley.*

> EXLEY
>
> Come on, Stensland, the party's upstairs.

*Stensland pushes past Exley, leading the cops into the lockup.*

INT. FRONT DOORS (HOLLYWOOD STATION) – NIGHT

*The Reporter and Photographer are returning.*

> REPORTER
>
> I know it's Christmas Eve. I just want to ask that kid Exley a few more questions.

*They stop short to watch as the cops push past Exley.*

INT. CELL BLOCK (HOLLYWOOD STATION) – NIGHT

*Stensland in the lead. Pulling out a BLACKJACK, he charges the cell where the Mexicans are being locked up.*

> STENSLAND
> For ours, Pancho. And you're getting off easy.

*He begins whaling on one of them—DINARDO. Cheered on by DRUNKS in the tank and his fellow officers, Stensland goes wild. Shaking his head, Jack Vincennes moves away.*

INT. SQUAD ROOM (HOLLYWOOD STATION) – NIGHT

*As Bud signs his REPORT, Jack looks in.*

> JACK
> White, you better get a leash on your partner before he kills someone.

INT. CELL BLOCK (HOLLYWOOD STATION) – NIGHT

*Followed by Jack, Bud forces his way through the crowd. The men who see it's him quickly clear a path.*

*Swigging from a pint of gin, Stensland works skinny GARCIA. Head saps. The Mexican drops to his knees drooling blood.*

*Bud hauls Stensland off. Drunk Stensland stumbles. Nose to nose, Bud tries to get through to him.*

                    BUD
    Stens . . . Hey, Stens . . .

*Bud's focused on Stensland as Garcia looks up at Bud.*

                   GARCIA
    Fuck you, *pendejo*.

                    BUD
    Yeah, yeah . . .

                   GARCIA
    And fuck your mother, too.

*Bud sees red, hauls Garcia up by the neck. There are CHEERS and "Attaboys" as Bud slams him high into the bars.*

                   EXLEY
                 *(arriving)*
    Stop, Officer! That's an order!

*Cops block Exley's way. Garcia takes an off-balance shot, which Bud responds to by shoving him aside.*

*Garcia stumbles out of the cell, smack into Jack. Jack*

*looks down aghast at blood on his cashmere blazer, then puts Garcia down with a left-right.*

*The floodgates are open. The drunks in the tank cheer as other cops start hitting and the Mexicans fight back. Police riot in the cell block.*

EXLEY
You're all going in my report!

*Two cops shove him off balance and hustle him into . . .*

INT. A STORE ROOM

*A cop slams the door tight. Exley is locked in. We hear him pounding.*

EXLEY'S VOICE
Let me out! That's an order!

*Exley moves to the small wire-mesh window that looks into the cell block and the ongoing melee. He pounds on the glass and yells.*

INT. CELL BLOCK (HOLLYWOOD STATION) – NIGHT

*The brawl continues unabated. The* Herald *Reporter and Photographer enter unchaperoned and unnoticed. Stensland swings like a madman. That's when a*

*FLASHBULB goes off. Freezing everyone in black & white.*

                                        DISSOLVE TO:


ESTABLISHING SHOT OF CITY HALL – DAY


INT. CITY HALL DET. BUREAU – THE CHIEF'S
OFFICE – DAY

*THE CHIEF sits behind a desk in a four-star uniform.
Dudley Smith sits to his left, politically savvy D.A. ELLIS
LOEW to his right, the only civilian. Bud White stands
across from them. There to be judged. The Chief holds
up a newspaper with Stensland's photo. The headline:*
BLOODY CHRISTMAS.

> THE CHIEF
>
> "Bloody Christmas." The press love to label.
> Officer White, you should know this is bigger
> than a police board. The grand jury is
> convening. Indictments may be handed down.
> Will you testify?

> BUD
>
> No, sir. I won't.

*The Chief sighs, looks to Loew.*

> THE CHIEF
>
> District Attorney Loew.

> LOEW
>
> You and Officer Stensland brought the liquor
> into the station. Stensland was already drunk.
> Do you see how appearing as a voluntary
> witness against him could offset the damage
> you've already done to yourself?

                    BUD
I won't testify against my partner or anyone
else.


                    LOEW
This man is a disgrace.


                  THE CHIEF
Your badge and gun, Officer.

*Bud sets them on The Chief's desk.*


                  THE CHIEF
You're relieved of duty pending termination.
Dismissed.

*Stone-faced, Bud White turns and marches out. Dudley
Smith watches after him with approval.*


INT. CITY HALL DETECTIVE BUREAU – HALLWAY –
DAY

*Exley approaches Bud coming the other way. Bud glares,
but Exley passes like he doesn't even see him.*


INT. THE CHIEF'S OFFICE (CITY HALL DET.
BUREAU) – DAY

*Dudley, Loew and The Chief face Exley.*

THE CHIEF
Ed, we need police witnesses to offset the
damage done to the department. I'm asking if—

EXLEY
The public demands justice, sir. Of course I'll
testify.

*The Chief and Loew exchange a look of relief.*

THE CHIEF
I'm glad you feel that way, Edmund. Most of
the men don't.

EXLEY
That's because they think silence and integrity
are the same thing.

*The Chief gestures with the Bloody Christmas newspaper
to Loew.*

THE CHIEF
Not exactly the image we're trying to create.

LOEW
*(sarcastically)*
Come to L.A., the City of the Future.

EXLEY
May I make a suggestion, sir?

THE CHIEF
By all means.


EXLEY
Shift the guilt to men whose pensions are secured. Force them to retire. But someone has to swing. Indict, try and convict Richard Stensland and Bud White. Secure them jail time. The public will see that your new LAPD will not tolerate men who think they're above the law.

*The Chief and Loew exchange a second look. Not bad . . . Dudley glares at Exley.*


DUDLEY
Richard Stensland is an embarrassment. Rotten fitness reports from every C.O. he ever served under. But Bud White is a valuable officer.


EXLEY
White's a mindless thug.


DUDLEY
No, Edmund. He's just a man who can answer yes to those questions I ask you from time to time.

*The Chief interrupts with his own concern.*

THE CHIEF

The department and the public need role
models. Clean cut, forthright men the public
can admire.
                    *(a beat; to Exley)*
Sergeant, I'll promote you. To lieutenant.
Effective immediately.

*Exley seizes the moment, going over Dudley's head.*

EXLEY

*Detective* lieutenant.

*The Chief and Dudley exchange a look. Neither approves.*

THE CHIEF

Ed, you're 30. Your father didn't make
lieutenant until he was 33.

EXLEY

I know that, sir. I also know that when he made
lieutenant, it was as a detective.

LOEW
                    *(interrupting)*
Before we start polishing our laurels, it would
look better if we had a corroborative witness.

DUDLEY

That'll be hard to come by. The men hate a stool
pigeon.

EXLEY

Jack Vincennes. He hit one of the Mexicans and
he saw the whole thing.

DUDLEY

A veteran like Vincennes might admit his own
culpability, but he would never inform.

*The Chief is on the verge of agreeing when Exley jumps
in.*

EXLEY

Jack's the technical advisor on *Badge of Honor*.
He lives for it. That's the way to get him.

THE CHIEF
*(into desk intercom)*
Call Sergeant Vincennes.
*(to Exley)*
I'd like you to observe, Ed.

*The Chief gestures toward a gray mirror on the wall. A
two-way. Exley nods. As he starts out, Dudley pulls him
aside, speaks low.*

DUDLEY

You'll reap the benefits, but are you truly
prepared to be despised within the department?

EXLEY

Yes, sir. I am.


DUDLEY

So be it.


INT. CITY HALL DETECTIVE BUREAU – NARCO PEN – DAY

*Looking sharp, Jack waits at his desk. A corkboard on the wall is posted with PRESS CLIPPINGS: "Dope Crusader Wounded in Shootout." "Actor Mitchum Seized in Marijuana Shack Raid." That one includes a shot of Jack ushering Mitchum into jail. As his phone rings . . .*


INT. THE CHIEF'S OFFICE (CITY HALL DET. BUREAU) – DAY

*Round three. Centered on Jack. Exley is watching behind the mirror.*


DUDLEY

Sergeant, we'll get right to it. Nine civilian witnesses have identified you as hitting Ezekiel Garcia.


LOEW

But my office has a stellar witness who will tell the grand jury that you hit back only after being hit.

JACK

And?

LOEW

You'll testify against three officers who have already earned their pensions. Our key witness will testify roundly, but you can plead ignorance to questions directed at the other men.

JACK

No thanks. I'm not a snitch.

THE CHIEF

I'll guarantee you a slap on the wrist. A brief suspension followed by a temporary transfer from Narcotics to Ad Vice.

*(a beat)*

When you transfer out of Vice, you'll be back on the show.

JACK

*(swallows)*

The show, sir?

THE CHIEF

*Badge of Honor,* Vincennes. We need to tone down your profile for a bit.

*The Chief just got Jack where he lives.*

                    DUDLEY
        John, I doubt you've ever drawn a stupid
        breath. Don't start now.


                     JACK
        Okay. I'll do it.


*Smiles all around. Loew smiles at the two-way. A move
not lost on Jack, who wonders who might be on the other
side.*


                  THE CHIEF
        Dismissed, Vincennes.


*Jack leaves. The Chief steps to the mirror, looks at it.*


                  THE CHIEF
        And so it goes . . . *Detective* Lieutenant.


OTHER SIDE OF THE GLASS

*Exley clenches his fist in victory. The Chief continues:*


                  THE CHIEF
        Ace them at the grand jury tomorrow, son.
        Wear a smart-looking suit and ace them. And
        Ed? Lose the glasses.

INT. COURTHOUSE – HALLWAY OUTSIDE GRAND
JURY ROOM – DAY

*Glasses off, Exley waits, sitting on a long bench. He looks
up as Jack approaches. People pass beyond them.*

> JACK
> You're the key witness?

> EXLEY
> That's right.

*Jack smiles, amused.*

> JACK
> I should've known. What's the Chief throwing
> you?

> EXLEY
> *Throwing me*?

> JACK
> Yeah, Exley. What's the payoff?

> EXLEY
> You're the payoff expert. I'm just doing my
> duty.

> JACK
> You're playing an angle, college boy. You're

getting something out of this so you won't have
to hobnob with the rank and file cops who'll
hate your guts for snitching. What is it,
downtown with the big boys, huh? If they're
making you a detective, watch out. Some
Bureau guys are gonna burn in this and you're
gonna have to work with friends of theirs.

                    EXLEY
What about you?


                    JACK
I'm snitching three old-timers who'll be fishing
in Oregon next week. Next to you I'm clean.
And smart.

*A GUARD steps out from a nearby room.*


                    GUARD
Edmund J. Exley to chambers.

*As Exley's about to go . . .*


                    JACK
Just remember, Bud White'll fuck you for this
if it takes the rest of his life.


INT. BOARDNER'S BAR – BOOTH – NIGHT

*On the jukebox, Chet Baker sings "Look for the Silver*

*Lining," as Bud slides into a booth opposite Dudley. A*
*NEWSPAPER is on the table, a little mound underneath.*

BUD
What do you want, Captain?

DUDLEY
Call me Dudley.

BUD
Dudley, what do you want?

DUDLEY
Lad, I admire your refusal to testify and your
loyalty to your partner. I admire you as a
policeman, particularly your adherence to
violence as a necessary adjunct to the job. And
I am most impressed with your punishment of
woman beaters. Do you hate them, Wendell?

BUD
*What do you want?*

DUDLEY
Wendell, I want you to come to work for me.

BUD
Doing what? Mowing your lawn?

*Dudley yanks the newspaper, revealing Bud's BADGE and .38 SPECIAL. Bud can't believe his eyes.*

                    DUDLEY
    They're yours. Take them.


                    BUD
    I knew you had juice, but there's no goddamn
    bill on me?


                    DUDLEY
    Four of the defendants recanted their
    testimony.

*Bud just stares at Dudley, who shrugs, smiles like the cat who ate the canary. Bud takes his gun and badge.*


                    BUD
    What about Stensland?


                    DUDLEY
    Your partner's through. Departmental
    scapegoat on the Chief's orders. He's been
    billed, he'll be indicted and he'll swing.


                    BUD
    *Exley.*

DUDLEY

Don't underestimate Exley or his skills. As a politician he exceeds even myself. The department needs smart men like Exley and direct men like you. I need you for an assignment the Chief's given me the go-ahead on. A duty few men are fit for, but you were born for. You'll be working out of Homicide at City Hall.

BUD

*(excited)*

Homicide? Working cases?

DUDLEY

Your talents lie elsewhere, Wendell. It's a muscle job. You'll do what I say and not ask questions. Do you follow my drift?

BUD

*(disappointed)*

In Technicolor.

DISSOLVE TO:

EXT. 1648 N. OGDEN ST. (HOLLYWOOD) – NIGHT

*Laughing, two MEN in flashy suits exit a house and cross the lawn to an OLDS 98 parked at the curb.*

HUDGENS' VOICE

Meet Tony Brancato and Tony Trombino, two
of Mickey Cohen's fast rising lieutenants. With
the dapper little gent in prison, who knows how
far they'll go?

*They climb into the front seat. The driver turns the key
and the RADIO comes on. SHOTS RING OUT, a cross fire
coming from two directions. The driver is hit through
the open window, and the passenger takes head hits
through the windshield. From the car radio, the pop
song "Hit the Road to Dreamland."*

HUDGENS' VOICE

Oh, well . . .

*MONTAGE BEGINS WITH ANOTHER ANGLE—Only this
one a still. Pull back to reveal the photo is on the front
page of the* Los Angeles Herald Express. *The headline
reads: MICKEY COHEN ASSOCIATES SLAIN IN HOLLY-
WOOD.*

INT. LADERA HEIGHTS HOUSE – NIGHT

*DEUCE PERKINS sits opposite another man in the spa-
cious living room of a modern house. On the coffee table
between them is a small suitcase and 25 pounds of
heroin.*

HUDGENS' VOICE

Meet Deuce Perkins, Mickey Cohen's narcotics

lieutenant. Could he be behind the hits? Is he consolidating gang power?

*Perkins licks his pinkie and dips it into the white powder. Sensing something, he looks up.*

*His POV through the plate window: on the other side of the lighted swimming pool, two dark figures are silhouetted against the lights of the city. There are two FLASHES of LIGHT, and holes appear in the plate window.*

*The man opposite Deuce Perkins is shot in the head. Deuce starts to stand. Two more shots shatter the window and knock Deuce over the couch.*

> HUDGENS' VOICE
> Guess not.

*As hands come in and scoop the suitcase of heroin from the table:*

> HUDGENS' VOICE
> One thing's for sure though, two-man triggers are punching the tickets on the Mickster's muscle.

EXT. THE VICTORY MOTEL – DAWN

*Set in the no-man's-land of the Baldwin Hills oil field. A broken neon sign features an oversized V, but nobody's triumphed here in years. Abandoned, but for a pair of LAPD cars, a light burning in room 5 and the sound of someone screaming.*

                    HUDGENS' VOICE
          Meanwhile, rumor has it the LAPD has set up a
          not-so-welcome wagon to discourage out-of-
          town visitors.

INT. THE VICTORY MOTEL – ROOM 5 – DAWN

*Spartan. A table and chair BOLTED to the floor. A tough FLATNOSED GANGSTER is cuffed to the hot seat.*

*On the table are a .45 and a fat roll of $100 bills. The studs are bare on one wall giving us a view of the adjacent room 6.*

*Strong-armed cops, BREUNING and CARLISLE, watch as Bud White delivers a series of short, stiff body shots. Flatnose is not used to being on the receiving end.*

*Dudley steps up behind Flatnose, makes himself heard.*

                         DUDLEY
          With Mickey Cohen in prison, Los Angeles is
          organized crime free. The Chief intends to keep
          it that way. Now, in Cleveland, you're an

organized crime associate in need of
reeducation in the ways of polite society.

*Flatnose babbles. Snitch-frenzied.*

FLATNOSE
I know things. I hear things. Like these two-
man shooter teams, bang-bang, they're 86-ing
Mickey Cohen's lieutenants. Or, or—You want
a prostie roust? Huh? Some narco action?

*(breaking down)*
What do you want?!

DUDLEY
We want you to go home.

*Dudley looks to Bud who applies more persuasion. Flatnose screams and we sense Bud's heart really isn't in this.*

*As "Hit the Road to Dreamland" ends, so does the montage.*

DISSOLVE TO:

ESTABLISHING SHOT OF CITY HALL – DAY

*The tallest building in the skyline, the seat of power.*

INT. CITY HALL DET. BUREAU – BRIEFING ROOM – DAY

*Addressing the squad, a no-nonsense VICE CAPTAIN picks up a stack of magazines.*

VICE CAPTAIN
Picture-book smut, gentlemen. There's been a bunch of it found at collateral crime scenes

lately. Quality ranges from piss poor to very well done.

*As the Vice Captain hands them out for the men to examine, new member Jack Vincennes arrives late.*

VICE CAPTAIN
Look who's back from suspension. We're honored, Sergeant Jack.

*The men laugh. Jack sits. Passing up the mags, he opens a leather "artist's" PORTFOLIO. Porno art shots. Men and women. Men and men. Girls and girls. Girls and horses.*

JACK
Gee. The Great Jerk-Off Caper of 1953.

VICE CAPTAIN
Vincennes, is there someplace you'd rather be?

JACK
Yeah, Cap. Back in Narcotics. Looking for Mickey Cohen's missing H.

VICE CAPTAIN
Yeah, finding twenty-five pounds of heroin would get you plenty of ink. Anyplace else?

JACK
Working whores with squad two.


VICE CAPTAIN
Maybe you should have thought of that before
Bloody Christmas. Make a major case, Sergeant.
It's the only way you're getting out of here.

*Exaggerated "oohs" and "ahhs" from the men.*


VICE CAPTAIN
Dismissed, gentlemen.


*As they go, Jack sees the portfolio is embossed on the
back with an elegant rendition of a fleur-de-lis. Jack
takes the matching business card from his wallet, the
one he found on Christmas Eve: "Fleur-de-Lis. Whatever you desire."*


VICE CAPTAIN
*(sarcastic)*
Go get the facts, Jack, "just the facts."


INT. CITY HALL DETECTIVE BUREAU – AD VICE
PEN – DAY

*Jack's new desk, no place to hang his clippings, which
sit in a box alongside the portfolio. Jack sits holding the
Fleur-de-Lis card. He dials the number. As it rings, he
leans a framed* Badge of Honor *photo up against his in/*

*out box: Jack and Brett Chase, before a banner that reads, To Protect and Serve.*

WOMAN'S VOICE
*(over phone; like silk)*
Whatever you desire.

JACK
Hi . . . I'd like to get a delivery to Beverly Hills.

WOMAN'S VOICE
I don't think I know you.

*CLICK. The line goes dead. Jack redials.*

WOMAN'S VOICE
Whatever you desire.

JACK
Look, a friend of mine gave me this number. I just —

*The line goes dead again. Jack dials a new number.*

OPERATOR'S VOICE
Pacific Coast Bell. Police line.

JACK
This is Sergeant Vincennes. Requesting a name

and address from the reverse directory.
Crestview 2–2–3–9.

>                    OPERATOR'S VOICE
> Please hold . . . No such number is assigned.

>                         JACK
> I just called it.

>                    OPERATOR'S VOICE
> No, Sergeant. I checked twice.

>                         JACK
>                  *(realizes; hangs up)*
> A bootleg . . .

*Jack dials another number.*


INT. *HUSH-HUSH* MAGAZINE OFFICE (SUNSET
BLVD.) – DAY

*Newspaper "page ones" stare down from the walls. Sid
Hudgens sits behind his desk, answers the phone.*

>                       HUDGENS
> *Hush-Hush,* off the record and on the QT.

>                     JACK'S VOICE
> Sid, it's Vincennes.

HUDGENS
Jackie, are you back on Narco? I need copy.

INTERCUT WITH JACK AT HIS DESK:

JACK
No. But I've got something going with Ad Vice.

HUDGENS
Something good for the Sidster?

                    JACK

Maybe. I'm chasing some porn. Kinky fuck
shots, but the posers don't look like junkies. It's
well done. Arty. I thought you might have heard
something.


                  HUDGENS

Not a word. Smut's from hunger, Big V. For sad
sacks who can't get their ashes hauled.


                    JACK

What about Fleur-de-Lis? Slogan's "Whatever
you desire."


                  HUDGENS

No, I've heard bupkis. Get me some Narco
skinny. I want to put out an all hophead issue.
Shvartze jazz musicians and movie stars.
Maybe tie it to the Rosenbergs. You like?


                    JACK

I'll talk to you later, Sid.


*Jack hangs up. A dead end. Jack tosses the portfolio into
a drawer. The drawer slides shut over the embossed
fleur-de-lis.*


INT. CITY HALL DETECTIVE BUREAU – HALLWAY –
DUSK

*Bud cools his heels, waiting outside a door beneath a
sign:* Internal Affairs.

INT. CITY HALL DET. BUREAU – INTERNAL
AFFAIRS – DUSK

*Dick Stensland turns in his badge and gun to an INTER-
NAL AFFAIRS DETECTIVE.*

INT. CITY HALL DETECTIVE BUREAU – HALLWAY –
DUSK

*Stensland joins Bud. Well-wishing DETECTIVES pat
Stensland on the back, offer words of encouragement.*

*Exley appears from the other end of the hall carrying a
box of stuff. It should be his big moment. But the same
Detectives wishing Stensland well stare daggers at
Exley.*

*Stensland starts for Exley. Exley braces himself, but
Stensland merely knocks the box from his hands, then
continues on.*

*As Bud passes Exley, following after Stensland:*

                    BUD
          Sorry about that, *Lieutenant.*

*The last door is* Homicide. *Exley continues, enters. . . .*

INT. THE SQUAD ROOM

*No greetings, just dirty looks. One detective whispers*

*something to another. The second detective looks at Exley, laughs. And as Exley searches for his desk . . .*


INT. CITY HALL – PARKING GARAGE – NIGHT

*Stensland and Bud reach Stensland's car. Stensland shrugs, opens the driver door.*


> STENSLAND
>
> Stay out of trouble, Bud.


> BUD
>
> I got a couple of hours before I have to be at the Victory. Want to grab a beer?


> STENSLAND
>
> Rain check me, partner. I got a hot date tonight.


> BUD
>
> Who is she and what did you arrest her for?


> STENSLAND
> *(smiles)*
>
> It's confidential. Like that magazine Vincennes scams for. *Hush-Hush.* Tomorrow night we'll do the town.
> *(winks)*
>
> On me.

BUD
Yeah? I'll bring my wallet just in case.

*Stensland gets in the car, drives off. Bud is left alone.*


INT. CITY HALL DETECTIVE BUREAU – SQUAD
ROOM – NIGHT

*Exley sits by himself in a sea of desks, his box of stuff unpacked. The SQUAWK BOX drones. He watches, listens as:*


DETECTIVE #1'S VOICE
See you tomorrow, Earl.


DETECTIVE #2'S VOICE
Wait, I'll walk out with you.

*Detective #2 pulls the last page of a report from a typewriter, joins Detective #1, who's leaving. Exley's ready to say good night, but they make a point never to look at him. They exit. Exley's alone.*

*Exley squints at the CLOCK on the wall, can't make it out. He takes his glasses from inside his jacket. 2:00 A.M. He checks his watch. 2:02. Finally, something to do. He walks to the wall clock, adjusts it two minutes.*

*As Exley sits, the squawk box booms to life.*

                         VOICE
          Anybody up there in homicide?

*Exley activates the lever on the squawk box.*

                         EXLEY
          Lieutenant Exley.

                         VOICE
          You've got a homicide. Downtown Division.
          Might be a multiple. The Nite Owl Coffee Shop.

                         EXLEY
          I got it. It's mine.

*Exley stands so fast he bangs his knee getting up.*

EXT. THE NITE OWL (DOWNTOWN) – NIGHT

*Patrol cars. Blues setting up a crime scene blockade. Exley
pulls up, douses his siren. PATROLMAN ONE runs over.*

                    PATROLMAN ONE
          At least one person dead. I stopped for coffee—

                         EXLEY
          No one comes through the front door. Got it?

*Exley pushes him aside, heads for the door.*

INT. THE NITE OWL – NIGHT

*Eerily quiet. Exley takes mental snapshots. Ten stools front a counter. The side wall mural-papered, winking owls perched on street signs. Behind the counter, a COOK sprawled dead, a .38 by his hand. The cash register is open and empty. On the left, a string of tables.*

*Three in disarray. Food spilled, dishes broken. A splatter of blood on the wall. A high heel pump by an upended chair.*

*A pair of heel drag marks and a thin trail of blood across the linoleum floor heading toward the rear. Exley follows. Outside—sirens. The trail leads out the rear door into . . .*

INT. THE BUILDING CORRIDOR

*Exley follows the trail of blood across the corridor that bisects the whole building to a men's room door. He pushes it open.*

INT. MEN'S ROOM – NIGHT

*Blood-soaked bodies on the cement floor. Five, maybe six in a tangle. Dozens of shotgun shells float in the pools of blood. As Exley struggles to maintain his composure, we hear the echoing sound of running footsteps coming down the corridor from the side street entrance.*

ROOKIE'S VOICE
Sir, there's a captain outside wants to see you.

*The Rookie looks into the men's room, blanches.*

EXLEY
Don't get sick! Not in here!

*Exley shoves the Rookie, puking, down the hall.*

EXT. THE NITE OWL – NIGHT

*Patrolmen hold back a swarm of reporters and rubber-neckers. Horns blast. Ed emerges, finds Dudley in command and barking orders.*

EXLEY
Sir, I took the call. It's my case.

DUDLEY
Edmund, you don't want it and you can't have it.

EXLEY
Yes, I do, sir.

DUDLEY
It's mine. I'll make you my second in command.

*Exley spots a PHOTOGRAPHER moving in. Taking off his glasses, he looks properly serious as the flashbulb pops.*

INT. THE NIGHT OWL – NIGHT

*Forensics Chief RAY PINKER walks Exley and Dudley through.*

PINKER
We got a total of fifteen spent 12-gauge

Remington shotgun shells. I figure three men with five-shot-capacity pumps.

*A FORENSICS COP approaches Pinker.*

> FORENSICS COP
> We got an ID on one of the victims, sir . . . It's Dick Stensland.

*Exley and Dudley react, look at each other.*

EXT. CORONER'S OFFICE. DAWN

*The Packard pulls up. Bud jumps out, runs for the entrance.*

INT. CORONER'S OFFICE – HALLWAY – DAWN

*Six sheet-covered bodies against the wall. Nite Owl victims. The CORONER lifts a corner of a sheet, gives an ORDERLY a peek of a WOMAN'S BODY we don't quite see.*

> CORONER
> Call me crazy, but for a second I thought it was Rita Hayworth.

*The Coroner follows as the Orderly wheels the corpse into an IDENTIFICATION ROOM.*

INT. (CORONER'S OFFICE) CLERICAL AREA – DAWN

*Exley stands with a few other COPS and CORONER AS-SISTANTS sipping coffee. Exley turns as Bud strides past and disappears down the hall.*

INT. (CORONER'S OFFICE) HALLWAY – DAWN

*Bud goes to the gurneys. Rips back three sheets before he finds him. Dick Stensland. A tag on his toe and half his face blown off. Stunned, Bud just stares.*

*Exley watches from down the hall.*

                    EXLEY'S VOICE
        Hell of a way to avoid a prison sentence.

*Bud turns, looks at Exley, trying to keep control. He squeezes out the words.*

                        BUD
        What happened?

                        EXLEY
        Appears three men held up a coffee shop. Guy
        at the register pulled a .38. They killed him and
        then took everyone else in the back and killed
        them, too.

*Then, from the identification room . . .*

CORONER'S VOICE
Lieutenant Exley, we're ready with that Nite
Owl ID.


INT. (CORONER'S OFFICE) IDENTIFICATION ROOM
– DAWN

*HILDA LEFFERTS, 50, has joined the Coroner to ID the
body of her daughter, Susan. There's stray buckshot in
the upper chest and shoulders, but a sheet hides the real
damage.*

*As Exley appears, Mrs. Lefferts looks confused.*


CORONER
Is this your daughter, Mrs. Lefferts?


MRS. LEFFERTS
I—I don't know.


EXLEY
We know this is difficult. Just take your time
and look again.

*Behind them, Bud has entered the room. Exley doesn't
realize, but Bud recognizes the deceased. It's the girl Bud
saw outside Nick's Liquor. Without the bandage and the
black eyes, she does look like Rita Hayworth.*

> MRS. LEFFERTS
Just before Christmas. We had fought. I didn't
like her boyfriend. I—She has a birthmark on
her hip.

*The Coroner lifts the sheet. Mrs. Lefferts gasps.*

> MRS. LEFFERTS
It's her. My baby.

> EXLEY
I'm sorry, Mrs. Lefferts.

*As Exley turns to go, Bud stops him.*

> BUD
Who's in charge of this investigation?

> EXLEY
Captain Smith and myself. Why?

*Bud doesn't answer. He goes out the door.*

INT. CITY HALL DET. BUREAU – BRIEFING ROOM –
DAY

*The room buzzes, jammed to the rafters with DETEC-
TIVES from every department standing ready. The Chief
waits as Dudley Smith takes the mike, holds up an L.A.
Times headline.*

                    DUDLEY
"Nite Owl Massacre." Hyperbole aside, this is a
heinous crime that requires a swift resolution.
The public will demand it and this department
will provide it. Six victims. One of them one of
our own—Dick Stensland.
                 *(the cops react)*
As it happens, he was a Nite Owl regular. In the
wrong place at the wrong time.

*Bud listens. Not so sure. Stensland said he had a date.*


                    DUDLEY
Robbery looks like the motive. We have rubber
glove prints on the register and preliminary
forensics strongly lean toward a trio of
gunmen. We do have one hot lead, so listen
well. Three Negro youths were seen last night
discharging shotguns in the air at Griffith Park.
A park ranger IDed them as driving a 1948 to
1950 Mercury coupe, maroon in color. An hour
ago a canvassing crew found a news vendor
who saw a maroon Merc coupe parked across
from the Nite Owl around 1:00 A.M.

*The room goes loud, a big rumbling. Dudley holds up a
list.*


                    DUDLEY
The DMV worked all night to get us a
registration list on '48 to '50 maroon Mercs.

There are 142 registered to Negroes in L.A.
County. Fifty two-man teams will shake three
names apiece. Hot suspects you'll bring here.
Interrogations will be run by Lieutenant
Edmund Exley.

*Catcalls. Boos. Exley, cleaned up, looks like he's slept
more than he has. The Chief steps to the mike.*

                    THE CHIEF
Enough on that. Gentlemen, just go out and get
them. Use all necessary force. The people of Los
Angeles demand it.

*The men exchange knowing looks. The real message: kill
them clean. Exley doesn't approve. As the men hurry
out . . .*

                    EXLEY
Why not just put a bounty on them?

INT. CITY HALL DETECTIVE BUREAU – SQUAD
ROOM – DAY

*Detectives pairing up and moving out. Scanning his
three-name list, Bud is joined by his PARTNER for the
day.*

                    PARTNER
Ready to roll, White?

                    BUD
You take them. I got something I gotta do.


                  PARTNER
Christ, I don't know. What if one of these
names . . .


*Off a look from Bud, the Partner nods he'll do it. Bud
heads off.*

*Exley watches everyone go. Wishes he could be part of
the action. He spots Jack talking to a BIG DETECTIVE,
who chews tobacco, has a Texas drawl.*


                BIG DETECTIVE
I got our assignment, Big V.


                    JACK
If we go by the list, we have about zero chance
of making the collar. But I know a guy who
knows what's going on South of Jefferson. I'm
betting he could put us at fifty-fifty.


                BIG DETECTIVE
I don't know . . .

*As Big Detective thinks, Exley steps up. He's overheard.*

                    EXLEY
I'll take those odds.
                    (to Big Detective)
Take off. We got it from here.

*Jack stares. The Big Detective shrugs, spits tobacco juice
in a cup.*

                    BIG DETECTIVE
Between the two of you guys, you should bring
along a photographer.


INT. NICK'S LIQUOR – DAY

*Last time we saw the Owner was Christmas Eve. He
looks up from a CUSTOMER as Bud strides in.*

                    BUD
I need an address on a customer of yours. Her
name is Lynn.

                    OWNER
That's all I have to go on?

                    BUD
Yeah. And I think you already know who I
mean, so cough it up.

                    OWNER
There's a billing address and a delivery address.

EXT. 416 DE MILLE DRIVE (LOS FELIZ) – DAY

*Bud White gets out of his car in a cul-de-sac high above the city. A sleek, modern architectural house spills down the hill from a street-level entrance. Approaching the house, Bud hears a distinctive sound and looks over the railing. On the lawn below, a tall, distinguished man, last seen outside Nick's Liquor on Christmas Eve, is chipping golf balls. They land in a tight grouping.*

BUD'S VOICE
You must slay 'em at the Country Club.

*Pierce Patchett turns and looks up.*

BUD
Are you Pierce Patchett?

PATCHETT
I am. Are you soliciting for police charities? The last time, you people called at my office.

*Bud just stares at him, shakes his head. Patchett considers, then, gesturing:*

PATCHETT
Go down to the driveway. We'll talk there.

EXT. 416 DE MILLE DRIVE (PATCHETT'S) –
DRIVEWAY – DAY

*As Bud approaches from the street, the garage door*

*slides up. Patchett steps out with his pitching wedge, cool as can be.*

PATCHETT

What can I do for you?

BUD

Where were you last night?

PATCHETT

I was here hosting a party.

BUD

Tell me about Richard Stensland.

PATCHETT

I don't know him, Mr. . . .

BUD

Officer White. How about Susan Lefferts? You know her?

PATCHETT
*(sighs; concedes)*
You know I do. You saw me with her. How did you find me?

BUD

Nick's Liquor. This is where Lynn Bracken's booze bills go.

                    PATCHETT
Of course . . .


                      BUD
Sue Lefferts died at the Nite Owl. I'm
investigating.


*Patchett studies Bud a beat, weighing his options. Pat-*

*chett's BURLY BODYGUARD appears in the doorway at the other end of the garage.*

BODYGUARD
Everything all right, Mr. Patchett?

PATCHETT
*(waves him off)*
Fine, Philip. Thank you.

BUD
Where's the other guy? *Buzz.*

PATCHETT
Buzz Meeks no longer works for me.

BUD
Lefferts looked beat-up Christmas Eve, but didn't act it. How come?

PATCHETT
I think she'd been hit in the face with a tennis racket. She is—was—a big doubles fan.

BUD
You're a known associate of a woman killed in a mass murder. You wanna go downtown and discuss this officially?

PATCHETT

Is that what this is? Official? Somehow I had
the feeling this was more personal with you.

*Bud doesn't answer, but the answer is yes.*

PATCHETT

All right. Do you care about criminal matters
peripheral to Susan's murder?

BUD

No.

PATCHETT

Then you wouldn't feel obligated to report
them?
*(off Bud's look)*
Then listen closely, because I'll only say this
once and if it gets repeated I'll deny it. I run call
girls. Lynn Bracken is one of them and so was
Susan Lefferts. I treat my girls very well. I have
grown daughters myself and I don't like the
idea of women being hurt. I sense you share
this feeling.

BUD
*(ignores comment)*
Why were Lefferts' eyes black?

PATCHETT

I needed a Rita Hayworth to fill out my little
studio.

BUD

What little studio?


PATCHETT

There's Gardner, Hepburn, Monroe, Turner.
Lynn Bracken is my Veronica Lake. I use girls
who look like movie stars; sometimes I employ
a plastic surgeon. When you saw us, the work
had just been done.


BUD

That's why her mother couldn't ID her . . . Jesus
fucking Christ.


PATCHETT

No, Mr. White, Pierce Morehouse Patchett.
Now I sense you're on your best behavior, but
that's all I'll give you. If you persist, I'll meet
you with my attorney. Now would you like
Miss Bracken's address? I doubt she knows
anything, but—


BUD

I got her address.


PATCHETT

Find Susan's killer, Mr. White. I'll give you a
handsome reward. *Whatever you desire.*

*Patchett smiles enigmatically, turns and walks through the garage toward the house. Bud is still watching him as the garage door slides down.*

EXT. 1736 ORANGE DRIVE, HOLLYWOOD (LYNN BRACKEN'S) – DAY

*A discreet Spanish house at the end of a street adjacent to a golf course. A projector's flicker strobes against the closed curtains. We hear a phone ring.*

INT. 1736 ORANGE DRIVE (LYNN BRACKEN'S) – DAY

*The film is* This Gun for Hire *with Alan Ladd and Veronica Lake. It's projected on a screen hanging from a banister, flashing over Lynn Bracken and an OLDER GENTLEMAN in his underwear. Lynn's long blonde hair hangs down over one eye. She looks more like Veronica Lake than Veronica Lake.*

*Lynn's on the phone, trying to listen as the older Gentleman embraces her from behind. She hangs up, turns to him.*

> LYNN
> You have to go. But I'll make it up to you. I promise.

> OLDER GENTLEMAN
> Gosh, kitten. I don't know . . .

*As he mashes up against her, there's a knocking at the door. Persistent. Lynn shakes her head, can't believe this.*

OLDER GENTLEMAN
*(as Alan Ladd)*
Is it the cops?

*He points his finger like Ladd points a gun, fires a couple of shots as Lynn goes to the door. She opens it to reveal Bud White.*

BUD
Miss Bracken, I'm Officer White—

*Bud stops short as he sees how she's dressed, then the half-naked Alan Ladd wannabe beyond her. Lynn is cool, acts like none of it's a big deal.*

LYNN
I've been expecting you. Just not this soon.
Pierce called. Told me what happened to Sue.

OLDER GENTLEMAN
Is everything okay, doll? Want me to get rid of
him?

BUD
Hit the road, gramps.

*Bud enters. The Older Gentleman strikes a pose. He still thinks he's Alan Ladd.*

OLDER GENTLEMAN
Maybe I will and maybe I won't.

BUD
*(flips a badge)*
LAPD, shitbird. Get the fuck out of here or I'll call your wife to come get you.

EXT. 1736 ORANGE DRIVE (LYNN BRACKEN'S) –
DAY

*Sputtering, the Older Gentleman exits with his clothes in hand.*

INT. 1736 ORANGE DRIVE (LYNN BRACKEN'S) –
DAY

*Bud looks the place over as Lynn shuts off the projector.*

> LYNN
> Can I get you a drink?

> BUD
> Yeah, Scotch. Straight.

*Bud watches her move to the bar. God, she's beautiful.*

> LYNN
> I was friendly with Sue Lefferts, but we weren't really friends. You know what I mean?

> BUD
> Are you sorry she's dead?

> LYNN
> Of course I am. What kind of question is that?

*She steps back with a Scotch for both of them.*

                    BUD
Have you ever heard of Dick Stensland? Stens?


                    LYNN
No, I haven't. Do you know why Pierce is
humoring you?


                    BUD
You use words like that, you might make me
mad.


                    LYNN
Yes. But do you know?


                    BUD
Yeah, I know. Patchett's running whores, and
judging by his address probably something
bigger on the side. He doesn't want any
attention.


                    LYNN
That's right. Our motives are selfish, so we're
cooperating.


                    BUD
Why was Susan Lefferts at the Nite Owl?


                    LYNN
I don't know. I never heard of the Nite Owl till
today.

BUD

Did Lefferts have a boyfriend?


LYNN

Like I said we were friendly, not friends.


BUD

How'd she meet Patchett?


LYNN

Pierce meets people. Sue came on the bus with
dreams of Hollywood. This is how they turned
out. Thanks to Pierce, we still get to act a little.


BUD

Tell me about Patchett.


LYNN

He's waiting for you to mention money.

BUD

You want some advice, Miss Bracken?


LYNN

It's Lynn.


BUD

Miss Bracken, don't ever try to fucking bribe

me or threaten me or I'll have you and Patchett
in shit up to your ears.

*Lynn smiles again.*

> LYNN
> I remember you from Christmas Eve. You have
> a thing for helping women, don't you, Officer
> White?

> BUD
> Maybe I'm just fucking curious.

> LYNN
> You say "fuck" a lot.

> BUD
> You fuck for money.

> LYNN
> There's blood on your shirt. Is that an integral
> part of your job?

> BUD
> Yeah.

> LYNN
> Do you enjoy it?

BUD

When they deserve it.


LYNN

Did they deserve it today?


BUD

Last night. And I'm not sure.


LYNN

But you did it anyway.


BUD

Yeah, just like the half dozen guys you screwed
today.


LYNN
*(laughs again)*

Actually, it was two. You're different, Officer
White. You're the first man in five years who
didn't tell me I looked like Veronica Lake inside
of a minute.


BUD

You look better than Veronica Lake. Now,
*Pierce Patchett*.


LYNN

He takes a cut of our earnings and invests it for

us. He doesn't let us use narcotics and he
doesn't abuse us. Can your policeman's
mentality grasp those contradictions?


BUD
He had you cut to look like Veronica Lake?


LYNN
No. I'm really a brunette, but the rest is me. And
that's all the news that's fit to print.

*Lynn starts toward the door. Bud watches her for a mo-
ment, then follows. She takes his glass at the door.*


LYNN
It was nice meeting you, Officer.

*Out the door, Bud turns back. Blurts:*


BUD
Look. I want to see you again.


LYNN
Are you asking me for a date or an
appointment?


BUD
*(suddenly unsure)*
I don't know.

                         LYNN
                    *(another smile)*
        If it's a date I think you'd better tell me your
        first name because I—


                         BUD
                    *(feeling foolish)*
        Forget I asked. It was a mistake.


*Lynn watches thoughtfully after Bud as he walks away.
He opens his car door like he's going to tear it off. A last
glance back at Lynn as he gets in the car . . .*


EXT. 9781 SOUTH DUQUESNE (SOUTH CENTRAL) –
DAY

*A BLACK BOXER pounds a heavybag/speed bag combo
bolted to the porch of the house. A wiry welterweight, he
doesn't see Jack and Exley till they're almost on top of
him.*


                         JACK
        Leonard Bidwell?


*The Boxer leans on the bag to catch his breath. Looking
them over, he finally nods.*


                         JACK
        How's the left these days?

                    BOXER
What's it to you?


                    JACK
I saw you fight Kid Gavilan. I like your style.


                    BOXER
What do you want, Mr. Policeman?


                    JACK
You got a brother up in Folsom. I know because
I put him there.


                    BOXER
Till 19-fucking-70.


                    JACK
How'd you like to make it 1960? I know the
Judge and Lieutenant Exley here is very good
friends with the D.A.

*They both look at Exley. He nods this is true. The Boxer's
still listening.*


                    EXLEY
We're looking for three colored guys who like to
pop off shotguns. One of them owns a maroon
Merc coupe.

BOXER

You wanna get me a fuckin' snitch jacket?


JACK

You wanna buy your brother ten years?
*(to Exley)*
It was ten years . . . ?


EXLEY

Yeah, ten years.


JACK

You don't have to say anything. Just look at this
list and point.

*Jack holds the DMV list out to the Boxer who waves
it off.*


BOXER

He's bad, so I'll just tell you. Sugar Ray Collins.
Drives a maroon '49 coupe, beautiful ride. Don't
know about shotguns, but he gets his thrills
killing dogs. He is righteous trash.

*Jack and Exley scan the list. Jack's finger stabs down on
Collins, Raymond, 9611 1/2 South Tevere.*


JACK

That's five minutes from here.

*As they take off:*

                         BOXER
        Hey. I'll hear from you, right? About my
        brother?


EXT. 9611 (SOUTH TEVERE ST.) – DAY

*A two-story house with garage apartments in back. Jack
coasts the car to the curb. He leaps out with Exley. Exley
holds up at the sight of a late model sedan. He leans
down to look in the window at the two-way on the dash.*


                         EXLEY
        It's one of ours.


                         JACK
        *Shit.* Someone beat us here.


*They run down the driveway of the house next door and
cut across. The door of one of the garages up ahead is
open, revealing a chrome bumper, a maroon fender.
Drawing a .38, Jack starts over. Exley, .38 in hand, follows.*


INT. 9611 (SOUTH TEVERE ST.) – GARAGE – DAY

*Toting shotguns, Dudley's boys from the Victory Motel,
Breuning and Carlisle, are looking into a '49 maroon
Mercury coupe. Jack and Exley come around the corner.*

JACK

Hey.

*Breuning wheels, pumps a round into the chamber. He very nearly fires before he sees who it is.*

BREUNING

What the hell are you guys doing here?

JACK
*(whispering)*
We were just in the neighborhood. What have you got?

*As Jack moves to peer through the Merc's window:*

CARLISLE
*(whispering)*
Three Ithaca pumps, an empty box of double-ought buck and some cash.

*Jack spots them. Three shotguns on the passenger side floor, an empty box of shells and loose dollar bills.*

JACK
So long, Vice, *Badge of Honor*, here I come.

*Carlisle explodes.*

CARLISLE
Fuck you, Vincennes! It's our collar.


EXLEY
Quiet! I'm ranking officer here. We go as a team.
End of story.

*Carlisle and Breuning look at each other, grudgingly nod assent.*

*Exley leads the way out.*


JACK
*(to Breuning)*
He's very serious.


INT. 9611½ (SOUTH TEVERE ST.) – STAIRWAY – DAY

*Breuning and Carlisle lead the way with Jack and Exley bringing up the rear. Squinting, Exley reaches to his pocket for something. Not there.*


EXLEY
Dammit . . .


JACK
What?

                    EXLEY

Glasses.


                    JACK
                *(chuckling)*
Just don't shoot me.


*The door to 9611½. Two men on either side. Breuning and Jack rear back. They kick at the same instant. The door flies off its hinges to reveal two young black men, RAY COLLINS and TY JONES, waking from a couple of flop mattresses.*


INT. 9611½ (SOUTH TEVERE ST.) – DAY

*Collins jumps up. Entering, Carlisle aims, but Exley hits his arm. The blast rips the ceiling. Jack aims.*


                    JACK

Freeze!

*Collins freezes. Jones doesn't dare get up.*


                    CARLISLE

Ace him, Jack.


                    EXLEY

Shut up, Carlisle!

*Breuning covers the two blacks, as Jack and Exley move for a closed bedroom door.*


                         EXLEY
              *(to Breuning, re: Collins and Jones)*
          Don't you kill them.

*Jack and Exley burst into a . . .*


INT. SECOND BEDROOM

*A black kid, LOUIS FONTAINE, in his underwear, going for the window. Fontaine flinches as Jack spins him, sticks his .38 in his back, starts to cuff him.*


                         JACK
                   *(winks to Exley)*
          So how does it feel to get out of the office?


INT. CITY HALL DET. BUREAU – OBSERVATION ROOM – DAY

*Dudley watches as Exley skims a report, memorizing names and dates. Jack reads the latest edition. Headline screams: NITE OWL ARRESTS. Other BRASS are here along with a STENOGRAPHER. Through tinted glass, the three suspects in three different interrogation rooms. As Bud enters, a LIEUTENANT waves him off.*

LIEUTENANT
It's crowded in here, White.


BUD
These guys killed Stensland.

*The Lieutenant relents, motions Bud in. Exley finishes skimming the report.*


EXLEY
"Casitas" . . . "Twenty-two" . . . "Burning clothes" . . .

*A UNIFORMED COP arrives, hands a report to Dudley.*


UNIFORMED COP
This just came up from forensics.

*Exley looks through the glass at the suspects, pauses at Fontaine, who looks young, vulnerable and scared.*

*Dudley hands Exley report photos—blow-ups of shell casings.*


DUDLEY
Hot off the press. The strike marks on shells fired from the suspects' shotguns match the strike marks on the shell casings found at the Nite Owl.
*(re: suspects)*

Ed, I want confessions. A night stewing ought
to have softened them up.


                         EXLEY
I'll break them, sir.


*As Exley steps into the first interrogation room, Jack
joins Dudley.*


                         JACK
You think golden boy is up to the task, Cap?


                         DUDLEY
I think you'll be surprised what Edmund's
capable of.


INT. INTERROGATION ROOM #1

*Exley closes the door. Ray Collins is cuffed to a chair.
One eye swollen shut, lip purple, a smashed nose with
one nostril split.*

*As Exley steps toward him, Collins pulls back warily.
Exley unlocks his cuffs, drops cigarettes and matches on
the table. As Collins rubs his wrists . . .*


                         EXLEY
They call you Sugar Ray because of Ray
Robinson?

(no answer)
They say Robinson can throw a four punch
combination in one second. Do you believe
that?

Collins just stares at him.


EXLEY
You're twenty-two, aren't you, Ray?


COLLINS
Say what and so what.


EXLEY
Did one of the officers work you over a little?

No bite. Collins just stares back.


EXLEY
So you're twenty-two, right?


COLLINS
Man, why do you keep asking me that?


EXLEY
Just getting my facts straight. Twenty-two
makes it a gas chamber bounce. You should
have pulled this caper a couple of years ago. Get
life, do a little Youth Authority jolt, transfer to

Folsom a big man. Orbit on some of that good
prison brew, get yourself a sissy—

                    COLLINS
I never truck with no sissies!


                    EXLEY
Louis . . . I almost believed him.


                    COLLINS
Believed what?


                    EXLEY
Nothing, Ray. You did the Casitas Youth Camp
with Louis, didn't you?


                    COLLINS
Man, why're you talkin' about Louis? His
business is his business.

*Unseen by Collins, Exley reaches under the table, takes
hold of one of three toggle switches.*


                    EXLEY
Sugar, Louis told me you went sissy up at
Casitas. You couldn't do the time so you found
yourself a big white boy to look after you. He

said they called you "sugar" because you gave
it out so sweet.

*Exley flips the toggle.*


INT. INTERROGATION ROOM #2

*The speaker over Louis Fontaine's head crackles to life.*

>                    COLLINS' VOICE
> Louis gave it out at Casitas! I was the boss
> jocker on my dorm! Louis's the sissy! Louis give
> it up for candy bars!


INT. INTERROGATION ROOM #1

>                    COLLINS
> He's got no more sense than a dog.

*Exley flips the toggle off.*

>                    EXLEY
> I heard you like to shoot dogs.

>                    COLLINS
> Dogs got no reason to live.

>                    EXLEY
> Oh? You feel that way about people, too?

COLLINS

Man, what're you saying?


EXLEY

Ray, we got the shotguns.


COLLINS

I don't own no shotguns.


EXLEY

Why were you throwing clothes in the building incinerator?


COLLINS
(trembling)

Say what?


EXLEY

You guys were arrested this morning, but none of you have last night's clothes. The building manager saw *you* throwing them into the incinerator. It doesn't look good.


COLLINS

I got nothin' more to say till I see a judge.


EXLEY

Were you on hop? You were passed out when you got arrested. Were you hopped up, Ray?

COLLINS

Ty and Louis fuck with that shit, not me.


EXLEY

Where do they get their stuff? Give me one to
feed the D.A. It'll make me look good, and I'll
say, "Sugar Ray isn't a punk like his sissy
partners."

*Collins hesitates, almost starts to speak. Exley flips up
the toggles as he leans in.*


EXLEY

All right, Raymond.


INT. INTERROGATION ROOM #3

*The speaker over Ty Jones's head crackles to life.*


EXLEY'S VOICE

. . . tell me just one more thing about Jones and
Fontaine. Where do they get their drugs?

*Jones reacts to his name.*


COLLINS' VOICE

Roland Navarette. Lives on Bunker Hill. He
runs a hole-up and sells red devils.

INT. OBSERVATION ROOM

*Watching the reactions of Jones and Fontaine through the glass, Jack looks to Dudley.*

                    JACK
     Exley's good. I'll give him that.


INT. INTERROGATION ROOM #1

*Exley flips down the switches, stands.*

                    EXLEY
     I'm going to take a break.

*Exley opens the door, looks back in afterthought.*

                    EXLEY
     You know, Ray, I'm talking about the gas
     chamber and you haven't even asked me what
     this is all about. You got a big guilty sign around
     your neck.


INT. OBSERVATION ROOM

*Exley enters from the first interrogation room.*

                    DUDLEY
     Masterful, Edmund. Your father would've been
     proud.

(pointing)
This one's on the verge.

*Exley looks through the glass into #2. Louis Fontaine—
weeping. A piss puddle on the floor by his chair.*

EXLEY
Fontaine's next, but give Jones the newspaper.
I want him primed.

*Exley heads for the door to #2. Dudley hands the paper
to a subordinate.*

DUDLEY
And take the cuffs off so he can read it.

INT. INTERROGATION ROOM #2

*Fontaine tries to control his sniffles as Exley enters.*

EXLEY
Louis, Ray Collins ratted you off. He said the
Nite Owl was your idea. You want to tell me
about it?

*No answer.*

EXLEY
I think it was Ray's idea. Talk and I think I can
save your life.

*No answer.*

EXLEY
Son, six people are dead and somebody has to
pay. It can be you or it can be Ray.

*No answer.*

EXLEY
Louis, he called you queer. He said at Casitas
you took it up the ass. He said—

FONTAINE
I DIDN'T KILL NOBODY!

*The voice is strong, full of conviction. Exley nearly
jumps back. He glances at the mirror, unsure. Then,
leaning in:*

EXLEY
Son, you know what's going to happen if you
don't talk. So for God's sake admit what you
did.

FONTAINE
*(sobbing)*
I didn't mean to hurt her. Maybe she's okay.

EXLEY
*Okay*? These people are all in the morgue. They
were dead when you left them.

FONTAINE
*(falling apart)*
I just wanted to lose my cherry. She don't die
so I don't die. She don't die so I don't die.

*Exley can't hide his surprise at this.*

EXLEY
Who are you talking about? Was she at the Nite
Owl? Who is she?

*But Fontaine is gone. Head lolling, eyes squeezing out
tears. The interrogation has taken a U-turn.*

INT. OBSERVATION ROOM

*Everyone watches, glued, as Exley exits Interrogation
Room #2 and heads for #3.*

INT. INTERROGATION ROOM #3

*Jones is reading the paper when Exley bursts in.*

JONES
This newspaper shit ain't shit.

EXLEY
Where's the girl Fontaine's talking about? Was
she a hooker? Did you kill her?

*No answer, but Jones looks nervous.*

                    EXLEY
You wanted Louis to lose his cherry, but things
got out of hand. Is that right?
                  *(no answer)*
Is she still alive?
                  *(no answer)*
Kick loose, Jones. I think you made her bleed.
She bled on your clothes, so you burned the
clothes.


                    JONES
Who told you that?!


INT. OBSERVATION ROOM

*Everyone's attention is riveted, particularly Bud's. They
watch, listen over the speaker.*


                    EXLEY
                *(over speaker)*
If that girl is alive, she is the only chance you've
got.


                    JONES
                *(over speaker)*
I think she's alive.


                    EXLEY
                *(over speaker)*
You *think*?

*No one notices as the chair back begins to splinter in Bud's hands.*

INT. INTERROGATION ROOM #3

*Exley leans over Jones, tries to wrap it up.*

> EXLEY
> Where is she now? Did you leave her
> someplace?
> *(no answer)*
> Did you sell her out? Give her to some of your
> buddies? Tell me where she is!

*The door blasts open. Bud slams Jones up against the wall. Pulling a .38, Bud breaks the cylinder, drops 5 shells on the floor.*

> BUD
> One in six! Where's the girl?!

> EXLEY
> Officer White, put down that weapon! I have
> this under control—

*Bud shoves the barrel into Jones' mouth, pulls the trigger twice. Click, click. Jones starts to slide down the wall.*

> BUD
> WHERE?!

*Exley grabs at Bud, who flings him back. Two more clicks. Jones spills:*

> JONES
> S-sylvester F-fitch one-o-nine Avalon, gray
> corner house, upstairs . . .

*Bud charges out, leaving Exley blinking in his wake.*

EXT. AVALON ST. – DAY

*A four-car cordon. They coast up to a GRAY CORNER HOUSE. Dudley Smith behind the wheel of the lead cruiser. Bud White rides shotgun, reloading his revolver.*

> BUD
> Give me one minute.

> DUDLEY
> You've got it, Wendell.

*Bud is out the door and scooting down the street toward the house. Exley moves to follow, but Dudley cuts him off.*

> DUDLEY
> We're going through the front.

EXT. BACKYARD. DAY

*Bud vaults a fence, pads up the steps to a back porch. A*

*screen door. Bud pulls a switchblade from his pocket. He slips the catch with the blade and steps inside.*

INT. FITCH APARTMENT – HALLWAY – DAY

*He silently moves down the narrow hall. Light seeps in from side rooms. We hear music and cartoon voices from up ahead. Bud looks into a . . .*

INT. BEDROOM

*A nude girl (INEZ SOTO) spread-eagled on a mattress. Bound and gagged. Her eyes grow wide at the sight of Bud, then flicker down the hall. Directing him.*

INT. HALLWAY – DAY

*Raising the .38, Bud continues along the hall. He looks into an empty kitchen. Up ahead . . .*

INT. LIVING ROOM – DAY

*SYLVESTER FITCH sits naked on the couch wolfing Rice Krispies and watching cartoons on a flickering TV. He looks up, sees the .38 before he sees Bud beyond it. Fitch sets down his spoon.*

*Bud shoots him in the face. Dead, Fitch just sits there.*

*Bud moves behind him. Pulling a spare piece from his*

*ankle holster, Bud fires back at the door from Fitch's line of fire, then puts the gun in Fitch's hand.*

*We hear a crash against the front door. As Fitch slides off the chair to the floor, Bud dumps the Rice Krispies on him.*

INT. STAIRWAY – DAY

*The front door flies open. Exley leads the charge up the stairs. A look in the living room tells the story. Dudley moves down the hall and looks into . . .*

INT. THE BEDROOM – DAY

*Bud is by the bed, covering the girl, comforting her and cutting the ties that bind.*

EXT. FITCH APARTMENT – DUSK

*Inez Soto on a stretcher. Being carried to an AMBU-LANCE. Bud White walks alongside, looking like some ferocious pet pit bull. The ATTENDANTS get her inside. One joins her. The other pauses to light a smoke.*

*Bud takes the cigarette from his mouth.*

> BUD
> Get her to the fucking hospital!

*One look at Bud, and the Attendant is running around to the driver's side.*

*Exley arrives, leans in to the rear of the ambulance.*

EXLEY
Miss, I'm Lieutenant Exley. I know this is difficult, but I need to know when they left you.

*Bud pulls Exley back.*

                    BUD
Give your career a rest and leave her alone.


*Bud closes the door, pounds the side of the ambulance,
signaling the driver to go. As the ambulance pulls out . . .*


                    EXLEY
A naked guy with a gun? You expect anyone to
believe that?


                    BUD
Get the fuck away from me.


*Bud starts away, Exley follows.*


                    EXLEY
How's it going to look on your report? Huh?


*Bud keeps going.*


                    BUD
It'll look like justice. That's what the man got.
*Justice.*


                    EXLEY
You don't know what the word means, you
ignorant bastard.

BUD
(stops; turns)
Yeah? You think it means getting your picture
in the paper.

*They're in each other's face. Other cops begin to take notice.*

BUD
Why don't you go after criminals for a change
instead of cops?

EXLEY
Stensland got what he deserved. And so will
you.

*Bud goes for Exley. Ten hands pull them apart. Dudley on Exley. Four cops genuinely having trouble on Bud.*

DUDLEY
You should stay away from a man when his
blood is up.

EXLEY
His blood's always up.

DUDLEY
Then maybe you should stay away from him
altogether.

*And, as if things couldn't get crazier, shouts from the cops on the street. Police radios cranked up:*

> DISPATCHER'S VOICE
> Repeat, three suspects escaped from the Hall of Justice jail. Raymond Collins, Ty Jones and Louis Fontaine. They are considered armed and extremely dangerous. Repeat, the Night Owl suspects have escaped . . .

INT. CITY HALL DETECTIVE BUREAU – SQUAD ROOM – NIGHT

*Electrified, "Nite Owl Killers" on everyone's lips.*

> COP ONE
> They jumped out a second floor window . . .

> COP TWO
> Girl at the hospital gave her statement. The three jigs left her at midnight. Plenty of time to be at the Nite Owl by one.

*Exley wades through it all, beelines the STENOGRA-PHER from the interrogation room.*

> EXLEY
> I need the interrogation transcript on Ray Collins.

> STENOGRAPHER

I'm typing it now.

> EXLEY

The question was, "Where do they get their drugs?" What was the answer?

*The Secretary scans her freshly typed pages, finds it.*

> STENOGRAPHER

"Roland Navarette. Lives on Bunker Hill. He runs a hole-up and sells red devils—"

*But Exley's already moving off. Police rush by.*

> EXLEY

Anyone seen Jack Vincennes?

*A few cops mumble they haven't. As Exley decides what to do, Carlisle from the original arrest steps over.*

> CARLISLE

Is something up, Lieutenant?

> EXLEY

I need some back-up . . . Come on.

EXT. VICTORIAN APT. BUILDING (BUNKER HILL) – NIGHT

*Exley and Carlisle pull up around the corner from a*

*four-story Victorian with paint peeling off the clap-boards.*

*They jump out of the car toting SHOTGUNS. They drop down over a wall and, dodging clothes on lines, cut through the narrow yards of a bungalow court.*

INT. VICTORIAN APT. BUILDING – STAIRWELL – NIGHT

*Carlisle waits as Exley checks the mail slots:* Navarette, 408. *Exley and Carlisle take the steps two at a time.*

INT. 4TH FLOOR HALLWAY (VICTORIAN) – NIGHT

*Exley squints, reaches to a pocket.* No glasses. *He passes an elevator, rounds a corner. There's 408. Exley pumps the shotgun, nods to Carlisle, who kicks the door in.*

INT. NAVARETTE LIVING ROOM (VICTORIAN) – NIGHT

*Exley and Carlisle burst in on four men eating sand-wiches. Fontaine and Caucasian NAVARETTE at a table. Collins on the floor. Jones by the window. No weapons in sight.*

EXLEY

Nobody move!

*Fontaine and Navarette raise their hands. A jostled beer bottle crashes to the floor.*

*Reacting, Carlisle jerks the trigger. Fontaine goes down.*

*Navarette draws a .38, shoots Carlisle twice in the chest. Exley blasts Navarette.*

*Screaming, Jones pulls a .45 from his belt. Exley fires, blowing him right through the window.*

*Collins makes a run for it out the kitchen door to the back door of the next apartment. Exley fires, taking out half the wall as Collins dives through the door.*

INT. EMPTY APARTMENT (VICTORIAN)

*Collins scrambles through, out the front door. Here comes Exley.*

INT. HALLWAY (VICTORIAN)

*Exley stumbles out, wiping Carlisle's blood from his eyes. Down the hall, he sees:*

*Collins vanishes into the elevator.*

*Exley charges as the elevator doors close.*

*The shotgun barrel juts through. The door bangs against it. BLAM!*

INT. ELEVATOR (VICTORIAN)

*The doors open and Exley stares down at what he's done.*

DISSOLVE TO:

*As Kay Starr belts "Wheel of Fortune," a MONTAGE begins.*

INT. CITY HALL DETECTIVE BUREAU – NIGHT

*Exley returns to grudging respect. His white shirt flecked with blood. He's clapped on the back by Dudley, who dubs him "Shotgun Ed." Exley doesn't enjoy it. He's numb, stumbling along. As he notices the blood on his hands . . .*

NEWSPAPER HEADLINE:

NITE OWL HERO! *Over a photo of Exley.*

EXT. CITY HALL STEPS – DAY

*Reporters scribble as The Chief speaks. Uniforms everywhere along with interested civilians.*

> THE CHIEF
> Edmund J. Exley has amassed a brilliant record
> in his seven years with the LAPD. Recently he
> evinced spectacular bravery in the line of duty.
> It is my pleasure to present him with our
> highest honor, the Medal of Valor.

*Exley steps up. The Chief hangs a gold medallion around his neck. Flashbulbs pop as the two men shake hands. The policemen stand on cue, applaud without enthusiasm.*

INT. VARIETY INTERNATIONAL PICTURES – STAGE 4 – DAY

*Cameras roll as Brett Chase interrogates a WITNESS*

*("Just the facts, ma'am."). Jack arrives to smiles and quiet handshakes. Someone hands him a script. Chase looks over, winks. Jack's back.*

EXT. 1736 ORANGE DRIVE (LYNN BRACKEN'S) – NIGHT

*Rain. A limo disgorges a HEAVYSET MAN who climbs the steps, knocks on the door. Lynn answers in an evening gown. He gives her a peck on the cheek and continues in past her. Lynn's about to follow him when she pauses to deadpan a look down the street.*

*Bud's Packard is parked there, his darkened silhouette behind the wheel. Smiling a bit sadly to herself, Lynn disappears inside.*

*This is no stakeout. Bud watches after her with yearning.*

INT. CITY HALL ROTUNDA – DAY

*Standing off to the side is the Older Gentleman last seen doing his best Alan Ladd impersonation at Lynn Bracken's. He stares emphatically at the SMARMY LAWYER who stands before him holding a manila folder.*

> OLDER GENTLEMAN
> You tell Mr. Patchett I have no intention of changing my vote.

*The Lawyer simply hands him a stack of photographs. From Lynn Bracken's apartment. The first is of the Older Gentleman naked except for his socks and garters.*

INT. CITY HALL – CITY COUNCIL CHAMBER – DAY

*The Older Gentleman rises for a council vote.*

> OLDER GENTLEMAN
> It may surprise some, but a mature man, enlightened by the facts, can change his mind . . .

EXT. FREEWAY GROUND BREAKING – DAY

*Pierce Patchett is among the distinguished guests. The Mayor is poised with a gold shovel.*

> THE MAYOR
> No stop signs. No traffic lights. From downtown to the beach in twenty minutes.

*As the Mayor scrapes at the ground . . .*

INT. BEVERLY HILLS HOUSE – NIGHT

*The monied JOHNS watch horny as hell as "GINGER ROGERS" twirls around the room with a female "FRED ASTAIRE." Clothes fly as they spin. Still most eyes turn* to Lynn Bracken as she enters, oozing that cat-girl grace. Surveying it all from a chair to the side—Pierce Patchett.

INT. VICTORY MOTEL – ROOM 5 – NIGHT

Screams. A CAULIFLOWER-EARED Cleveland mob EN-FORCER on the hot seat. Breuning works him with a rubber hose as Dudley asks unanswered questions. Bud watches, revulsion growing.

> DUDLEY
> Where did you intend to start? Prostitution? Gambling?
> *(no answer)*
> Go back to Jersey. This is the City of Angels and you haven't got any wings.

As the hose thwops down, Bud looks away, leaves the room.

INT. BATHROOM (VICTORY MOTEL) – NIGHT

Bud runs water in the sink to drown out the screams. It doesn't work. He leans down and sticks his head under the stream of water. That doesn't work either.

EXT. VICTORY MOTEL – NIGHT

Hair dripping wet, Bud makes it to his car. The tires spit

*gravel as he tears away. Dudley appears in the doorway, watching curiously. As the song "Wheel of Fortune" concludes . . .*

INT. BUD'S PACKARD – 1736 ORANGE DRIVE
(LYNN'S) – DAWN

*Bud watches Lynn Bracken's apartment. Colored lights play on the windows. Shadows pass. As the front door opens, there's Veronica Lake, all sparkles and spangles, kissing another DISTINGUISHED GENTLEMAN good-night.*


INT. LIVING ROOM – 1736 ORANGE DRIVE – DAWN

*Now Lynn just looks tired. As she puts away Scotch bottles and picks up empty glasses, there's a knock on the door. Lynn sighs, becomes sultry Veronica Lake before our eyes.*


INT. FRONT HALL – 1736 ORANGE DRIVE – DAWN

                    LYNN
                *(opening door)*
        Did you forget some—

*Bud stands there, filling the door frame.*


                    LYNN
        I wondered when you might knock on my door
        again, Officer White.


                    BUD
        It's Bud.

*Bud looks at Lynn a moment, then down at his own feet. Embarrassed. She smiles.*

                          LYNN

Bud . . .


INT. LYNN'S ROOM – 1736 ORANGE DRIVE – DAWN

*The door opens to a small, simply furnished bedroom.
The effects are personal, nothing of Veronica Lake. Bud
takes it in, looks at Lynn. She smiles slightly, almost
shyly.*

                          BUD

Why me?


                          LYNN

I'm not sure.

*Bud takes her in his arms. He loosens her dress at the
waist. She lets it fall. Naked in more ways than one. As
she starts to undress Bud . . .*


INT. CITY OF ANGELS HOSPITAL – VISITOR'S
LOUNGE – DAY

*Among the gathered PRESS, a PHOTOGRAPHER checks
his camera as a REPORTER waits.*

                        REPORTER

Good story. Rape victim wheeled out of hospital
by the man who killed the guys who did it.

PHOTOGRAPHER

Yeah . . . Pulitzer stuff.

INT. CITY OF ANGELS HOSPITAL – HALLWAY – DAY

*Exley wheels the rape victim (Inez Soto) along.*

INEZ

Thanks for what you did. For killing those *putos* who raped me.

*(a beat)*

Will you thank Officer White for me?

EXLEY

Sure . . .

INEZ

Seeing him come through the door is about the only thing I remember. Thank god.

*This bothers Exley.*

EXLEY

But you remember what time the Negros left you. In your statement, you said they left you at midnight.

INEZ

They might have.

> EXLEY
> *(stops)*

Might have?

> INEZ

I don't know when they left me. I wanted them dead. Would anyone have cared that they raped a Mexican girl from Boyle Heights if they hadn't killed those white people at the Nite Owl? I did what I had to for justice.

*As Exley's head swims . . . Up ahead, the press have spotted them.*

INT. VARIETY INTERNATIONAL PICTURES – STAGE 4 – NIGHT

*A* Badge of Honor *fund-raiser for a CITY COUNCIL-MAN'S reelection campaign. Hot dogs and sauerkraut. Fishbowls stuffed with cash. Jack is here, returns a glad-hander's greeting. D.A. Ellis Loew sits on one side of the Councilman, the Councilman's WIFE and TEENAGE DAUGHTER sit on the other as actor Brett Chase speaks.*

> BRETT CHASE

This election is about the future of law enforcement in Los Angeles. A friend of the police, City Councilman Rogers represents that future. So dig deep, and let's get a moral man reelected. District Attorney Ellis Loew would like to say a few words.

*Applause. Leaving the podium, Brett Chase is replaced by Loew. Chase smiles at the Councilman's daughter, who absolutely gushes. Chase then winks knowingly to Jack.*

*Jack scans the room, checks himself out in a mirror.*

> HUDGENS (O.S.)
> Big V Jack Vincennes!

*Jack turns to see Sid Hudgens approaching.*

> HUDGENS
> Good to see you're back, boychick.

> JACK
> Sid, how are they hanging?

> HUDGENS
> Down around my ankles. You tight with the D.A., Jackie?

> JACK
> Sure, he just tried to throw me off the force last Christmas as a joke.

> HUDGENS
> How about some payback big time? Not to

mention a donation to the widows and orphans
fund. Did you know Loew was a swish?

JACK

No kidding?

*Hudgens scans the crowd, points someone out.*

HUDGENS

You remember Matt Reynolds? "The Movie
Premiere Pot Bust"?

*Jack spots Matt Reynolds—one of the young actors he
arrested on Christmas Eve.*

HUDGENS

He just got off the honor farm.

JACK

What's he doing here?

HUDGENS

Reynolds's acey-deucey. Not to mention broke.
I'm getting him to fuck the D.A. for a hundred
bucks.

*(winks)*

That's twice the fifty you got for wrecking his
career.

*Even Jack's not immune to a comment like that.*

                         HUDGENS
    Matt! Over here!


                          JACK
    No, Sid . . .


*As Reynolds arrives, Hudgens points out . . .*


                         HUDGENS
    That's D.A. Loew right there.


*Reynolds gets a nervous bead on Loew. Hudgens realizes:*


                         HUDGENS
    You need a drink, Kid . . . Jack, look after him a
    minute. Kid, this is Jack. No secrets between
    me and him.


*Hudgens heads off. Reynolds, pale, nods at Jack.*


                        REYNOLDS
    Have we met before?


                          JACK
    Yeah.


*Jack doesn't really feel like talking to him. Reynolds'
nerves won't let him stay quiet.*

REYNOLDS

Was it a party?


JACK

Something like that.


REYNOLDS
*(misreading)*
A Fleur-de-Lis party, right?


*Jack remembers the name, plays along for what it's worth.*


JACK

Fleur-de-Lis. "Whatever you desire."


REYNOLDS

Dope, hookers that look like movie stars. Pierce Patchett has it all.


JACK
*(bluffing along)*
You got that right.


REYNOLDS

He isn't like regular people. I dig him, but he scares me, too.

                         JACK
     Really? How?

*Reynolds is staring at D.A. Ellis Loew.*

                       REYNOLDS
     You know, when I came out to L.A., this isn't
     exactly where I saw myself ending up.

                         JACK
     Get in line . . .

*Reynolds looks like he's going to cry. Hudgens returns
with a double Scotch straight up and a hot dog with sauerkraut. He hands the drink to Matt.*

                       HUDGENS
     Dutch courage, kid. Drink up.

*Reynolds downs a few gulps, looks across the room at
Loew.*

                       REYNOLDS
     I don't know if I should do this.

                       HUDGENS
     Hey, it's not like you don't know how. And Jack
     here has connections on *Badge of Honor.* Pull
     this off and there'll be a part for you. I smell a
     comeback. Don't you, Jack?

*Reynolds looks to Jack, who gives a noncommittal shrug.*

                    HUDGENS
          Loew's free. Go introduce yourself.

*Reynolds looks toward Loew, hesitates.*

                    HUDGENS
          Talk to him, Jack. Tell him about the opening
          on the show.

                    JACK
I'm pretty sure I can get you a part on the show
. . . But tonight? Just pretend it's an acting job.
Showbiz.


                    REYNOLDS
And no one'll know about this?


                    HUDGENS
No.


                    JACK
It'll be our secret.


                    REYNOLDS
Showbiz . . .


*Emboldened by Jack's promise, Reynolds drains his glass and heads off.*


                    HUDGENS
If Reynolds works his charms, which he will,
they'll be around the corner at the Hollywood
Center Motel. Room seven. Meet me at
midnight for a little photo shoot. Maybe we'll
work in the Hollywood sign this time.


*Hudgens holds out a President Grant $50 bill. Jack doesn't take it.*

JACK

Sid, what do you know about Pierce Patchett?

HUDGENS

Patchett? Why do you ask?

JACK

I've been hearing some rumors. Wild parties,
high-class porn. Hookers that look like movie
stars.

HUDGENS

Jackie, all I know is what you know. The man
is very rich. And he's invested in freeway
construction, so he's gonna get a lot richer. But
that's it. Patchett's what I like to call
"Twilight." He ain't queer, he ain't Red, he
can't help me in my quest for prime sinuendo.

*Jack takes the $50. Jack and Hudgens watch as Reyn-
olds strikes a conversation with Loew, who's captivated.*

HUDGENS
*(laughing)*
As though *Badge of Honor* would touch that kid
with a ten-foot pole after he's been the *Hush-
Hush* cover boy twice in one year.

*Hudgens chomps a bite of his hot dog, gives Jack the high
sign, but Jack just feels like a pimp.*

>                    JACK
>              *(starts away)*
> I'll catch up with you in a couple of hours.


>                  HUDGENS
> Midnight. I guarantee all kinds of illegal
> activity.


                                        CUT TO:


INT. MOVIE THEATER – NIGHT

Roman Holiday *on the screen. A humorous moment between Gregory Peck and a radiant Audrey Hepburn. Among those in the packed house: Bud and Lynn. She watches the screen, laughing, but he can't stop looking at her.*


EXT. FROLIC ROOM (HOLLYWOOD BLVD.) – NIGHT

*A hole-in-the-wall. Next door, at the Pantages,* The Bad and the Beautiful *is playing.*


INT. FROLIC ROOM. NIGHT

*The BARTENDER walks down the bar to where Jack stares into his empty glass. Dino is on the jukebox.*

BARTENDER

Another, Jack?


JACK

Yeah.

*The Bartender pours. The bill Jack pulls out is the FIFTY
Hudgens gave him. The things he's done for fifty bucks
. . . He looks at his reflection in the bar mirror. Is that*

*him? Jack checks the clock. 11:15. With sudden resolution, Jack drops the fifty on the bar and leaves.*


EXT. HOLLYWOOD CENTER MOTEL (SUNSET BLVD.) – NIGHT

*Jack pulls up. He gets out and heads with purpose for room 7. The TV's on inside. Loud. Jack knocks.*

                    JACK
        Kid? Matt?


INT. HOLLYWOOD CENTER MOTEL – ROOM 7 – NIGHT

*Jack opens the door. Next to the bed is a body. Matt Reynolds. Soaked in blood. Throat slit. Reynolds seems to stare back at him as Jack looks down in horror.*


INT. 1736 ORANGE DRIVE, LYNN'S ROOM. NIGHT

*Spent, Bud and Lynn lie in bed. She is passive, lost in thought.*

                    BUD
        All they get is Veronica Lake. I get Lynn
        Margaret Bracken.

*Lynn looks over, smiles. He's read her mind. Bud*

*changes the subject by picking up a pillow. A tasseled job with a cactus and an embroidered "Bisbee, Arizona."*

BUD

Bisbee?

LYNN

I grew up there.
*(a beat)*
Couple years I'm going back and open a dress shop. The girls in Bisbee need a little glamour.

*Bud looks back to the pillow. He smiles, then starts to laugh.*

LYNN

What's so funny?

BUD

Bisbee. It's almost as bad as Wendell.

*They share a laugh.*

LYNN

Nothing wrong with Wendell. Nothing wrong with Bisbee either.

*Lynn's finger traces a scar on Bud's shoulder.*

> LYNN
>
> Where'd this come from?

> BUD
>
> When I was twelve, my old man went after my mother with a bottle. I got in the way.

> LYNN
>
> So you saved her.

> BUD
>
> Not for long.

*A bitter memory.*

> LYNN
>
> I'm sorry, Bud. It's—

> BUD
>
> He tied me to the radiator. I watched him beat my mother to death with a tire iron. He left me there with her. Three days till a truant officer found us. They never found the old man.

*They look at each other a moment. Lynn reaches out, touches his face. Bud starts to pull back, but then lets her do it.*

> LYNN
>
> Is that why you became a cop, Bud? To get even?

                    BUD

I don't know. Maybe.


                    LYNN

Do you like it?


                    BUD

I used to. Now it's all strong-arm, sitting duck
stuff.

*Lynn waits, knows there's more.*


                    BUD

There's something wrong with the Nite Owl.
That prick Exley . . . he shot the wrong guys.
Whoever killed my partner is still out there.

*Frustrated, Bud pokes at his own chest.*


                    BUD

In here I know it. But I can't prove it. I'm not
smart enough. I'm just the guy they bring in to
scare the other guy shitless.


                    LYNN

You're wrong. You found Patchett. You found
me. You're smart enough.

*There's conviction in her voice and Bud hears it.*

INT. CITY HALL DETECTIVE BUREAU – FORENSICS
LAB – DAY

*Burgeoning with files and boxes of evidence. A size 16
facility in a size 8 dress. Ray Pinker looks up from his
microscope as Bud enters.*

PINKER

Bud White, what brings you down to the
basement?

BUD

I got a few Nite Owl questions.

PINKER

I don't know if you read the papers, but that
case is closed.

BUD

Anything bother you about it?

*Pinker gestures to a pile of evidence loaded in cardboard
boxes and manila envelopes. All are marked "Nite Owl"
with the case number.*

PINKER

Yeah. The fact that the pack-up boys haven't
hauled this shit out of here yet.

*Pinker goes back to his microscope. Undaunted, Bud*

*steps over to the pile of evidence, picks up the crime scene photos.*

PINKER

I got three shotguns, taken from the suspects, which match the strike marks on the shell casings. What more do you want?

*Among the photos is one which includes the wall next to one of the tables. There is a small spatter.*

BUD

There's blood on the wall. I thought they all got shot in the men's room.

PINKER

It's Stensland's blood.

BUD

Stensland?

PINKER

He took a blow to the head. Was probably unconscious when they dragged him into the john.

BUD

Did they hit anyone else?

PINKER

No. But he was a cop. He probably tried to do
something.

*Bud checks out the tables in the photo, looks close.*

BUD

Grilled cheese, black coffee . . .

*Bud points out there are two coffee cups on the table,
sees a lipstick smear on one of them.*

BUD

Someone was sitting with him. How many of
the victims were women?

PINKER

Two. Patty DeLuca, the late-shift waitress and
Susan Lefferts.

*Bud looks back at the photo, puts a finger on the table
between the two coffee cups.*

BUD

Susan Lefferts.

PINKER

What about her?

*Bud doesn't answer. He's out the door.*

PINKER

You're welcome.


EXT. LEFFERTS' HOUSE (ELYSIAN PARK) – DAY

*A shingle shack dump. Bud rings the bell. Hilda Lefferts answers. She doesn't look so good.*


BUD

Mrs. Lefferts, I'm Officer White with the LAPD. I'd like to ask a couple of questions.


MRS. LEFFERTS

Let my daughter rest in peace.


BUD

Five minutes. That's all.


INT. LEFFERTS' HOUSE – LIVING ROOM – DAY

*Pictures of Susan smile down from four walls. Vamp poses on a nightclub floor. Mrs. Lefferts is all twitchy and nervous, her eyes darting to a closed door.*


BUD

Tell me about the boyfriend she had. The one you mentioned at the coroner's office.

                    MRS. LEFFERTS
First I want to go on record as saying that my
Susie was a virgin when she died.


                         BUD
Ma'am, I'm sure she was.

*Mrs. Lefferts talks directly to a photo of her daughter.*


                    MRS. LEFFERTS
Susie, I told you I didn't approve of that
boyfriend. He was too old for you. You let him
be fresh to me.
                    *(to Bud)*
They came here one day when I wasn't home.
Old Mrs. Jensen next door saw Susan's
boyfriend and another man and she heard a
ruckus.


                         BUD
What was the boyfriend's name?


                    MRS. LEFFERTS
We were never properly introduced. Susan
called him by a nickname. Muns or Lunts or
something.


                         BUD
Stens? Was it Stens?

>                    MRS. LEFFERTS
> Maybe. I don't know.


>                          BUD
> Look at a picture for me.

*Bud hands her Stensland's photo ID.*


>                    MRS. LEFFERTS
> That's him. That's him.


>                          BUD
> You said a neighbor heard a ruckus. Was it
> outside, inside?


>                    MRS. LEFFERTS
> Outside. Mrs. Jensen said they kept going under
> the house.

*Bud catches the look Mrs. Lefferts throws to the closed
door. Rolled towels are crammed against the bottom of
the door.*


>                    MRS. LEFFERTS
> You'll have to leave now, Officer.

*Bud starts for the closed door.*


>                          BUD
> What's through here?

> MRS. LEFFERTS
> Just a room full of old things . . .

*Bud kicks away the towels, opens the door, steps into . . .*


INT. A BEDROOM

*Innocuous except for the smell. It hits Bud right off.*

> MRS. LEFFERTS
> Don't mind the smell. I think a rat died behind
> the wall . . .

*Bud's eyes are on the floor.*

> MRS. LEFFERTS
> My Susie was a good girl!

*As Mrs. Lefferts goes shrill, Bud beelines out the door.*


EXT. LEFFERTS' HOUSE – DAY

*Holding a flashlight, Bud crawls under the house,
into . . .*


INT. THE CRAWLSPACE UNDER HOUSE

*Bud elbow-crawls over the dirt, between wood pilings.*

*There's a long burlap sack up ahead. It smells bad. Bud*

*rips burlap. A rat's nest explodes. As the rats clear, he sees a gristle-caked human skull staring back, a crack in the forehead.*

*Undaunted, Bud tears the burlap back further. He pats the corpse's pockets, comes up with a WALLET. Bud checks the ID.* Leland Meeks. *Bud knows him by that name and another.*

> BUD

Buzz Meeks . . .

EXT. LEFFERTS' HOUSE – DAY

*Bud crawls out, blinking sunlight and gulping fresh air. Mrs. Lefferts is there. She's scared.*

> MRS. LEFFERTS

Was it . . . a rat?

> BUD

Yeah. A great big one.

*Bud opens Meeks' wallet, pulls out some bills and gives them to Mrs. Lefferts.*

> BUD

Here. Compliments of the Los Angeles Police Department.

INT. CITY HALL DETECTIVE BUREAU – SQUAD
ROOM – DAY

*Exley sits staring at the Medal of Valor he holds in his
hand. It's time to decide. Finally, he does. As Exley returns the medal to a drawer . . .*

INT. CITY HALL DETECTIVE BUREAU – FORENSICS
LAB – DAY

*Two STOREROOM TYPES are loading boxes of Nite Owl
evidence onto a dolly when Exley enters. Seeing Exley,
Pinker gestures to the coroner's report he's holding.*

>                    PINKER
> Stomach of the week from a motel homicide.
> Frankfurters, sauerkraut, Coca-Cola, alcohol
> and sperm. Jesus, what a last supper.

*As Pinker chuckles, Exley isn't amused.*

>                    EXLEY
> The Nite Owl. Anything bothering you about
> that case?

>                    PINKER
> Yeah. The fact that you guys won't let it get
> filed away.

>                    EXLEY
> What are you talking about?

                    PINKER
Bud White grilled me on it this morning. You
know, he's not as dumb as I thought.

*Exley's head swims.*

                    EXLEY
Do you know where he was going when he left
here?


EXT. LEFFERTS' HOUSE (ELYSIAN PARK) – DAY

*Mrs. Lefferts waters the grass, watches as a car pulls up.
Exley gets out, starts toward her. She drops the hose and
runs for the front door. Exley cuts her off.*

                    MRS. LEFFERTS
Let my Susie rest in peace!


                    EXLEY
Mrs. Lefferts, I just want to ask a few
questions.


                    MRS. LEFFERTS
Officer White already checked under the house
and found not a thing amiss.


                    EXLEY
Under the house? Where?

MRS. LEFFERTS
Around back. All he found were rodents!


INT. CORONER'S OFFICE – AUTOPSY ROOM – DAY

*Exley walks alongside as a body bag is wheeled into the autopsy room atop a gurney. The Coroner steps over.*


EXLEY
I need an ID ASAP. You talk only to me on this one.


INT. CITY HALL DETECTIVE BUREAU – NARCO PEN – DAY

*Jack sits brooding at his desk. An issue of* Hush-Hush *before him, the "Movie Premiere Pot Bust" on the cover. Jack barely notices as Exley steps up.*


EXLEY
Vincennes, I need your help with something.


JACK
I'm kind of busy right now, Lieutenant. Take it up with one of your boys in Homicide.


EXLEY
I can't. I need someone outside Homicide. I

want you to follow Bud White. Until he goes on
duty tonight.

### JACK

Why don't you do me a real favor and leave me
alone?

*Exley hesitates, looks around.*

### EXLEY

Do you make the three Negroes for the Nite Owl
killings?

### JACK

What?

### EXLEY

It's a simple question.

### JACK

You should be the last person who wants to dig
any deeper into the Nite Owl case, *Lieutenant.*

### EXLEY

Rollo Tomasi.

### JACK

Is there more to that, or do I have to guess?

                    EXLEY
Rollo was a purse snatcher. My father ran into
him off duty. He shot my father six times and
got away clean. No one even knew who he was.
I made the name up to give him some
personality.


                    JACK
So what's the point?


                    EXLEY
Rollo Tomasi is the reason I became a cop. I
wanted to catch the guys who thought they
could get away with it. It was supposed to be
about justice. But somewhere along the way I
lost sight of that . . . What about you, Jack?
Why'd you become a cop?

*Jack looks like he might cry, but smiles instead.*


                    JACK
I don't remember . . .

*Both men are quiet a moment.*


                    JACK
What do you want, Exley?


                    EXLEY
I just want to solve this thing.

                    JACK

The Nite Owl was solved.


                    EXLEY

I want to do it right.


                    JACK

Even if you pay the consequences?

*Exley nods. Jack looks at him a beat, gets up.*


                    JACK

Okay, college boy, I'll help. But there's a murder
your boys in Homicide think is just another
Hollywood *Homo*cide. I don't. I'll help you with
yours, you help me with mine. Deal?


                    EXLEY

Deal.

*Jack nods. They're partners.*


EXT. THE FORMOSA (SANTA MONICA BLVD.) – DAY

*A Packard pulls up out front. Bud gets out, heads inside.
Another car pulls up across the street.*


CLOSE ON JACK

*Watching Bud. Jack gets out, starts across the street.*

INT. THE FORMOSA – THE BAR – DAY

*At the bar, Johnny Stompanato looks over as Bud joins him. Stompanato isn't happy about it, but he smiles anyway.*

> STOMPANATO
> Wendell White, how's tricks, *paesano*?

> BUD
> I ain't your *paesano*.

*Bud puts a twenty-dollar bill on the bar.*

> STOMPANATO
> And I ain't in the snitch business no more.

> BUD
> You remember an ex-cop named Buzz Meeks?
> He works for a guy named Patchett.

> STOMPANATO
> Should I?

> BUD
> He's muscle for hire, you're muscle for hire.

> STOMPANATO
> Oh yeah, Buzz Meeks. A rundown ex-cop. Same

as you're going to be some day. That's all you're
going to get, and you can keep your twenty
bucks.

*Bud's hand flashes out, grabs Stompanato by the crotch.*

> BUD
> What do I get if I give you your balls back, you
> wop cocksucker?

*Stompanato doubles over, his face almost on the bar.*
*The words come out in gasps:*

> STOMPANATO
> There was a rumor going around that Meeks
> had a line on a large supply of H.

*Bud squeezes harder.*

> BUD
> And?

> STOMPANATO
> And nothing.

> BUD
> Bullshit. Where would a two-bit hick like
> Meeks get a large supply of heroin?

                    STOMPANATO
     I don't know!

*Bud loosens his grip. Stompanato gasps for air.*


INT. (THE FORMOSA) – THE DOOR – DAY

*Jack peeks in, catches a glimpse of Bud and Stompanato, too far away to hear anything.*


INT. (THE FORMOSA) – THE BAR – DAY

*Stompanato's recovering.*

                    STOMPANATO
     You're probably right, it is bullshit. Besides,
     even if he had it, he could never unload it. Not
     without drawing all kinds of attention.

                        BUD
     Maybe that's why he's under a house in Elysian
     Park and he don't smell too good. *Paesano* . . .

*Bud sticks the twenty in Stompanato's pocket and leaves.*


EXT. 1736 ORANGE DRIVE (LYNN BRACKEN'S) – DUSK

*Jack pulls up, sees Bud knock on the front door. The door opens and Bud goes in.*

EXT. BUSHES – OUTSIDE 1736 ORANGE DRIVE
(LYNN'S) – NIGHT

*Leaves rustle; movement in the underbrush. Jack appears, followed by Exley. They get a partial view through a window.*

*Bud White sits on a footstool massaging a pair of women's feet. Jack and Exley exchange a curious look. This isn't the Bud White they're used to. A pair of women's hands reach out to Bud, the arms covered in glitter and satin.*

*The woman, Lynn Bracken, leans forward to kiss her policeman. It may have been a long day, but she's every inch Veronica Lake. Exley reacts.*

> JACK
>
> Maybe Bud White's not so dumb after all.

*They stand, kiss again. Lynn's gown spills down around her ankles. Bud scoops Lynn into his arms and the two of them disappear up the stairs.*

EXT. CARS – A BLOCK FROM 1736 ORANGE DRIVE
– NIGHT

*Exley and Jack walk to their cars.*

> EXLEY
>
> Rita Hayworth at the morgue and now Veronica Lake with White. What the hell's going on?

JACK

I'm not sure, but I think your case and my case
are connected. It's Fleur-de-Lis again.


EXLEY

Fleur-de-Lis?


JACK

"Whatever you desire." Porno, high-line
whores with plastic surgery to look like movie
stars. Who knows what else? Reynolds, the kid
who was killed, was involved. So's Pierce
Patchett.


EXLEY

The millionaire?


JACK
(nods)
I think we should go talk to him.


EXLEY

First I want to brace Stompanato.


INT. THE FORMOSA (SANTA MONICA BLVD.) –
NIGHT

*The place is jumping. Lee Wiley's singing "Looking at
You" from the jukebox.*

*Exley and Jack enter, scan. There's Stompanato in a booth with a woman who looks amazingly like "LANA TURNER." Engrossed, Stompanato doesn't react till Exley's nearly on top of him. Jack follows.*

STOMPANATO
Hey, you want an autograph, write to M-G-M.

EXLEY
Since when do two-bit hoods and hookers give out autographs?

STOMPANATO
*What*?

*As Stompanato stands, Exley flashes his badge. Jack takes a look at "Lana."*

EXLEY
LAPD. Sit down.

"LANA"
Who in the hell do you think you are?

JACK
Ed—

EXLEY
*(to "Lana")*
Take a walk, honey, before I haul your ass downtown.

"LANA"
WHO IN THE HELL DO YOU THINK YOU
ARE?!

JACK
Ed—

STOMPANATO
You are making a large mistake.

"LANA"
Get away from our table!

*Exley leans down.*

EXLEY
A hooker cut to look like Lana Turner is still a
hooker. She just looks like Lana Turner.

JACK
She is Lana Turner.

EXLEY
What?

JACK
She *is* Lana Turner.

*Lana tosses her drink in Exley's face.*

EXT. THE FORMOSA – NIGHT

*Grim, Exley follows Jack across the street.*

EXLEY
How was I supposed to know?

*They get in Exley's car. Exley takes off his glasses, wipes them with his handkerchief. Jack starts to laugh. A moment, then Exley starts to laugh as well.*

EXT. 416 DE MILLE DRIVE (PATCHETT'S) – NIGHT

*Exley's Ford is parked on the street.*


INT. 416 DE MILLE DRIVE (PATCHETT'S) – LIBRARY – NIGHT

*In a silk robe, the unflappable Pierce Patchett smiles at Exley.*


                    PATCHETT
     I believe the Nite Owl is your area of expertise,
     Mr. Exley. I saw you on television getting your
     medal.
                    *(turns to Jack)*
     And you're that other celebrity Hollywood
     policeman?

*Jack draws an imaginary six gun.*


                    EXLEY
     The Veronica Lake look-alike works for you.
     She's one of your whores, correct?


                    PATCHETT
     A vulgar term.


                    EXLEY
     Why is she seeing Bud White?

PATCHETT
Why do men and women usually see each other,
Mr. Exley?

*There is something suggestive, insinuating, in his
manner.*

JACK
How about Fleur-de-Lis? An actor named Matt
Reynolds?

*Patchett frowns at Jack like he's speaking Chinese.*

EXLEY
We want answers, Patchett.

PATCHETT
We all want something.

EXT. 416 DE MILLE DRIVE (PATCHETT'S) – NIGHT

*Exley and Jack head for the car.*

JACK
Guy's as cool as they come.

*A call crackles in over Exley's radio. Exley picks up.*

EXLEY
This is Exley.

DISPATCHER'S VOICE
The Coroner wants to talk to you, Lieutenant.
Says he has your ID.

EXLEY
Tell him Sergeant Vincennes is coming in to talk
to him.
(to Jack)
I'll drop you at your car.

JACK
Where are you going?

EXLEY
Lynn Bracken's. I'm going to find out why
Patchett has her seeing Bud White. I'll meet you
at the Frolic Room.

JACK
Great. You get the girl; I get the coroner.

INT. 416 DE MILLE DRIVE (PATCHETT'S) – LIBRARY
– NIGHT

*Watching Exley and Vincennes from the window, Patchett picks up the phone and dials.*

HUDGENS' VOICE
(over phone)
*Hush-Hush*, off the record and on the QT.

INT. CORONER'S OFFICE – AUTOPSY ROOM –
NIGHT

*Jack is with the Coroner.*

> CORONER
>
> God bless dental records. Stiff used to be a cop.
> Leland Meeks.

> JACK
>
> *Buzz* Meeks?

> CORONER
>
> You knew him?

> JACK
>
> Of him. He was around when I first joined the
> force. A bad rep.

*As Jack leaves:*

> CORONER
>
> "Just the facts," Jack, just the facts.

INT. CITY HALL DET. BUREAU – RECORDS ROOM –
NIGHT

*Jack looks up from a personnel file as a female CLERK
approaches.*

                         CLERK
Anything else, Sergeant?


                          JACK
Leland Meeks worked Ad Vice from '39 to '41.
Let me see his arrest records.


INT. 1736 ORANGE DRIVE (LYNN'S) – LIVING ROOM
– NIGHT

*The lighting is low, the mood romantic. Jackie Gleason's
recording of "But Not for Me" is on the hi-fi. There is a
knocking on the door. Lynn opens it to reveal Exley.*


                         EXLEY
Miss Bracken, I'm Lieutenant Exley.


                          LYNN
I know who you are. Bud told me all about you.

*As he enters:*


                         EXLEY
Is that so? And what did White say?


                          LYNN
He said you were smart. He also said you were
a coward. That you'd screw yourself to get
ahead.

EXLEY

Let's concentrate on my smarts. Pierce Patchett
made you, didn't he? He taught you how to
dress and talk and think, and I am very
impressed with the results. But I need some
answers and if I don't get them, I'm going to
take you and Patchett down.

LYNN

Pierce Patchett can take care of himself and I'm
not afraid of you.

*She walks up close to him, looks in his eyes.*

LYNN

And you forget one thing, Lieutenant. Pierce
also taught me how to fuck.

*She smiles at him, walks away, deeper into the house.
Exley follows.*

EXLEY

And he tells you who to fuck. Why does he have
you fucking Bud White?

LYNN

What makes you think I'm not seeing Bud
because I want to?

*Exley scoffs.*

                    LYNN
It would be easier for you if there was an angle,
wouldn't it? You're afraid of Bud because you
can't figure how to play him. He doesn't follow
the same rules of politics as you do. It makes
him dangerous.


                    EXLEY
I can handle Bud White.


                    LYNN
Can you?

*She advances on Exley. He becomes increasingly aware
of her plunging neckline, her beauty . . .*


                    LYNN
I see Bud because I want to. I see Bud because
he can't hide the warmth he has inside him. I
see Bud because he makes me feel like Lynn
Bracken and not some Veronica Lake look-alike
who fucks for money. I see Bud because he
doesn't know how to disguise who he is. I see
him for all the ways he's different than you.

*Exley's voice is hushed and a little hoarse.*


                    EXLEY
Don't underestimate me, Miss Bracken.

> LYNN
> The way you've underestimated Bud White?

*Exley's had it. Lost to himself, Exley leans in and kisses her. Lynn pulls back.*

> LYNN
> Fucking me and fucking Bud aren't the same thing you know.

> EXLEY
> Stop talking about Bud White.

*He kisses her again. She kisses back. In a beat they're rolling to the floor shedding clothes. Lynn looks over his shoulder at her reflection in a closet door mirror. Or is she looking past that?*

INT. CLOSET

*Behind two-way glass. Sid Hudgens snaps pictures as Lynn and Exley continue their frantic lovemaking . . .*

EXT. FROLIC ROOM (HOLLYWOOD BLVD.) – NIGHT

*Jack exits, checks his watch, looks both ways up and down the boulevard.*

EXT. 9608 VENDOME, SILVERLAKE (DUDLEY'S HOUSE) – NIGHT

*Jack's Studebaker is out front. He rings the bell of the*

*dark house. The porch light comes on. The door opens to reveal Dudley Smith in his bathrobe.*

DUDLEY
John Vincennes. It's nearly midnight, lad.

JACK
Two minutes, Dudley. It's important.

DUDLEY
Lucky for you that my wife and four fair daughters are at the beach in Santa Barbara.

INT. 9608 VENDOME, (DUDLEY'S) KITCHEN – NIGHT

*Jack sits at the table. Dudley reheats coffee at the stove.*

JACK
You remember Buzz Meeks, Dudley?

DUDLEY
A disgrace as a policeman. What about him?

JACK
Twelve years ago he worked a vice roust with Dick Stensland. They questioned Pierce Patchett on a blackmail scam. Patchett had Sid

Hudgens photographing prominent
businessmen with hookers. Charges were
dropped. Insufficient evidence. You were
supervising officer on the case and I was
wondering if you remember anything about it?

DUDLEY

What's this all about, lad?

JACK

Part of it has to do with a murder. I've been
working with Ed Exley on it.

DUDLEY

You're Narco, lad, not Homicide. And since
when do you work with Edmund Exley?

JACK

It's a private investigation. I fucked something
up and I want to make amends.

DUDLEY

Don't start trying to do the right thing, John.
You haven't had the practice.

*Dudley walks over, hands Jack his coffee.*

DUDLEY

Buzz Meeks and Dick Stensland. What does Ed
Exley make of all this?

                    JACK
I haven't told him. I came straight from the
records room.

*Without warning, Dudley raises a revolver. He fires it at
point-blank range right into Jack's heart. Jack reacts,
eyes wide with surprise, then resignation. Dudley
crouches down beside him.*

                    DUDLEY
Have you a valediction, lad?

*Jack opens his mouth to speak. His lips form words, but
no sound comes out. Dudley leans low, gives Jack an
ear.*

                    JACK
Rollo Tomasi.

*Dudley frowns in ignorance at the name.*

*Jack smiles to himself, then dies.*


INT. CITY HALL DET. BUREAU – BRIEFING ROOM –
DAY

*Nothing mobilizes the police department like losing one
of its own. Dudley is at the podium. A dazed-looking
Exley is off to the side. Dozens of DETECTIVES take
notes, including Bud White.*

                    DUDLEY
Sergeant Vincennes was killed by a single .38
round to the heart. Although he was found in
Echo Park, preliminary forensics indicate the
body may have been moved. I want two-man
teams to scour the area. That means knocking
on every door. Jack Vincennes was one of our
own, gentlemen. Justice must be swift and
merciless. That is all.

*As the men move off, Dudley stops Exley.*

                    DUDLEY
Edmund, a word with you. We're trying to get
a lead on an associate of Vincennes. A records
check has reached a dead end.

                    EXLEY
What's the name?

                    DUDLEY
Rollo Tomasi.

*Exley tries to hide his reaction as Jack calls to him from
the grave. Screaming the name DUDLEY!*

                    DUDLEY
Have you ever heard Vincennes mention him?

                         EXLEY
No. No, I haven't.


                        DUDLEY
It may be nothing, but keep your ears open.

*As Dudley moves off, Exley watches him go.*


INT. CITY HALL DETECTIVE BUREAU – NARCO –
DAY

*Bud is standing over an impatient DETECTIVE's desk.*


                          BUD
But supposing, just supposing someone did
have that much heroin, who would they go to
to move it?

*Dudley, striding through the Bureau, calls out:*


                        DUDLEY
White! In my office. Now!

*Bud turns.*


                          BUD
Yes, sir.
            *(he turns back to the detective)*
Just give me a name.

DETECTIVE
All right . . . Mickey Cohen.

*Exasperated, Bud leaves.*

INT. CITY HALL DET. BUREAU – DUDLEY'S OFFICE
– DAY

*Bud knocks on the door, and Dudley waves him in.*

DUDLEY
Close the door, lad. You're perplexing to me
these days, Wendell. You're not your old cruel
self anymore. And I had such plans for your
future.

BUD
What plans?

DUDLEY
You have your extracurricular activities and I
have mine. We must hold a clarification session
soon. But for now, I need your fearsome old
habits at the Victory Motel. We're going to
brace a man who may know who killed Jack
Vincennes. Can I count on you?

BUD
Yes. Yes, you can.

INT. CORONER'S OFFICE – AUTOPSY ROOM – DAY

*The Coroner looks up as Exley enters.*

> EXLEY
>
> I want to know everything and anything you
> and Jack Vincennes talked about last night.
> Start with the ID on the corpse.

> CORONER
>
> An ex-cop. Leland "Buzz" Meeks.

*Exley's wheels are turning.*

> EXLEY
>
> An ex-cop? Did Jack know him?

> CORONER
>
> Only by reputation.

INT. VICTORY MOTEL – DAY

*A rainstorm has turned the courtyard into a mud bath.
As usual a light burns in room 5. Bud White parks alongside the other cars already there. He makes a dash for
the door.*

INT. VICTORY MOTEL – ROOM 5 – DAY

*Sid Hudgens is in the hot seat. Dudley sits across from*

*him. Dudley's henchman, Breuning, is cuffing Hudgens to the chair.*

DUDLEY
This is Mr. Hudgens, Wendell.

HUDGENS
I'm happy to cooperate. You don't need to tie me down.

DUDLEY
It's for your own safety. Now what can you tell us about Sergeant Jack Vincennes?

HUDGENS
Hollywood Jack? The Big V? I can tell you he's on the Night Train to the big adios.

*Breuning belts Hudgens on the side of the head.*

HUDGENS
Hey! I didn't have anything to do with him getting killed if that's what you mean.

DUDLEY
But you were business associates?

HUDGENS
What does that have to do—

*Breuning hits him again.*

                    HUDGENS
Okay! Okay! So we worked together. It was an
information exchange. I got him first-class
collars and he got me good stories. We were
friends for Chrissakes!


                    DUDLEY
All right. We'll drop that line for now. Next
topic. Please comment on Pierce Patchett.

*Bud looks over at mention of the name.*


                    HUDGENS
You think Patchett had something to do with
Vincennes getting iced?

*Dudley sighs, looks to Bud.*


                    DUDLEY
Wendell. I want full and docile cooperation on
all topics.

*Hudgens flinches as Bud steps up, twice Breuning's size.*


                    HUDGENS
Okay. Okay. Everyone knows Patchett's worth
a boatload of greenbacks. From aviation to
freeway construction. But the man has hobbies,
too. He bankrolls B movies under the table. And
try this on: he's rumored to be a periodic heroin

sniffer. All in all, a powerful behind-the-scenes strange-o.

DUDLEY

And?

HUDGENS

And what?

*Bud digs a fist into Hudgens' gut. As Hudgens gasps to get his breath back:*

DUDLEY

Reciprocity, Mr. Hudgens, is the key to every relationship.

HUDGENS
*(gasping for air)*
He runs call girls. Primo tail. Fixed up to look like movie stars.

*Bud looms, rests his hands on the back of Hudgens' chair. He doesn't like where this is going.*

DUDLEY

And?

HUDGENS
In my car. Blackmail shit. In the trunk under

the carpet. Patchett got me to photograph a cop
fucking this gorgeous piece of tail Lynn, looks
just like Veronicaaa—

*Wooden slats pop as Bud rips the bolted chair up with
the floorboards. Hudgens and the chair land sideways
leaving a hole behind in the floor.*

                    DUDLEY
        Wendell!

*Bud can't hear him. He uprights the chair one-handed.
As his fist cocks back, he's restrained by Breuning and
Dudley. This is no act. They can barely hold Bud back.*

                    HUDGENS
        Get him away from me!

*Dropping Sid, Bud breaks free, heads outside.*

EXT. VICTORY MOTEL – HUDGENS' CAR – DAY

*Bud jams a tire iron into the trunk seam and pops it with
a ferocious yank. He tears at the carpeting. A manila
envelope. Bud rips it open and 8 × 10 glossies of Exley
and Lynn spill out. Raindrops dot them.*

INT. VICTORY MOTEL – ROOM 5 – DAY

*Dudley and Breuning watch from the door as Bud
speeds away in his Packard.*

DUDLEY

I wouldn't trade places with Edmund Exley
right now for all the tea in China.

*Breuning smiles. Hudgens, still cuffed to the chair up-
ended on the floor, calls from behind them:*

HUDGENS

Dudley . . . Dudley, I thought you were gonna
let the dumb bastard kill me.
*(to Breuning)*
And you! Learn to pull those punches better.

*Dudley and Breuning stare at him. A bit grimly.*

HUDGENS

You can uncuff me now, fellas.

*But no one moves to do so.*

HUDGENS

Fellas?
*(nervous)*
Dudley, we had a deal. You, me, and Patchett.
We're a team!
*(scared)*
Come on, we're friends. We're—

*Dudley slaps a hand over his mouth.*

DUDLEY

*Hush-Hush . . . .*


INT. CITY HALL DETECTIVE BUREAU – RECORDS
ROOM – DAY

*Exley watches as a FEMALE CLERK searches dusty fil-
ing cabinets filled with Arrest Records dating from the
late thirties to the early forties. She looks up.*


EXLEY

So Buzz Meeks made no arrests from 1939 to
'41?


CLERK

Someone must've pulled the files.

*Exley ponders the implications.*


EXLEY

I want to look at the old duty rosters.


CLERK

The duty rosters? If we still have them, they're
buried in the basement somewhere.


EXT. 1736 ORANGE DRIVE (LYNN BRACKEN'S) –
DAY

*Blue, Lynn sits on her porch watching the rain come*

*down. A screeching on the wet street as Bud's Packard pulls up. She watches as he gets out and starts for the house. Lynn stands, holds her arms out. Bud stops short, out of reach, the rain soaking him.*

BUD

Did you talk to Exley?

LYNN

Come in out of the rain.

*Lightning flashes. Bud shakes his head.*

BUD

I want to know about Exley.

LYNN

He's the opposite of you. He's more like me.

BUD

How'd you get to know so much about him?

*More lightning. Lynn looks god-awful sad.*

LYNN

Come in out of the rain, Bud.

BUD

You gonna tell me what happened with you and Exley?

                           LYNN
We talked.


                            BUD
So tell me about it.


                           LYNN
                      *(looking away)*
Later. Just come in.


                            BUD
No. Now.
                        *(a beat)*
You fucked him.


                           LYNN
I thought I was helping you. I thought—

*Bud backhands her hard. Lynn faces straight into the next one as Bud hits her again. The third time takes her down as the sins of the father are visited on the son. Bud stops short as the self-realization slams home. She doesn't start crying till Bud turns and runs away into the rain.*


INT. CITY HALL DETECTIVE BUREAU – RECORDS ROOM – DAY

*Exley flips through old duty rosters. Sign out sheets on*

*patrol cars. On July 27, 1938, Dick Stensland in car 6. Exley slides a finger over to the name of his partner that day: Leland Meeks! Listed on top, the watch commander: Sgt. Dudley Smith! Exley ripples through the following weeks. The three names linked together time after time.*

*Exley looks up at the sound of footsteps as Bud comes through the door.*

EXLEY

White. I'm glad you're here . . .

*Bud holds it up for Exley to see: a crumpled glossy of him and Lynn.*

EXLEY

Wait—

*Bud slams Exley, knocks him flat. He's here to kill him. He hauls Exley up, pummels him, then throws him over a table. The FEMALE CLERK jumps up, flees out the door. Bud and Exley ricochet down the narrow aisle of file cabinets, then hit the floor. Bud tries to shove the photo down a gagging Exley's throat.*

*Exley's flailing hand finds Bud's .38. Yanking it from his waistband, Exley smashes Bud in the forehead. Bud reels, falls. As he gets up, he's looking down the barrel of the .38.*

EXLEY

Listen to me. Dudley killed Jack. He wanted
you to kill me.
(re: photo)
Dudley showed you that, didn't he? Didn't he?

Bud slaps the gun away, drops Exley to the ground. He
begins slamming his head into the floor.

EXLEY

Think, goddamn you! Think . . .

Exley's almost out. But maybe Bud heard him. The at-
tack slows, switches gears as Bud releases Exley and
takes his rage out by knocking over several filing cabinets.

Exley stays conscious, looks on as Bud masters himself.
The door opens revealing two DETECTIVES and the female clerk.

BUD

Stay the fuck out of here!

He slams the door. Bud's eyes are on the photos of Lynn
on the floor.

BUD

Dudley . . .

EXLEY

I checked the duty rosters. Dudley and Buzz
Meeks and Stensland go way back.

*Bud is not surprised. More like resignation.*

BUD

I knew Stensland lied to me. Lefferts' mother
IDed Stensland as Lefferts' boyfriend, but Stens
pretended he didn't know her or Meeks the
night I met Lynn.

EXLEY
*(sitting up)*

Stensland and Meeks. What the hell were they
up to?

BUD

I don't know. But I think it had something to do
with heroin.

EXLEY

What heroin?

BUD

Johnny Stompanato told me that Meeks had a
line on a large supply of heroin. Meeks ends up
dead. Stensland dies at the Nite Owl.

> EXLEY
>
> It wasn't the Negroes. The rape victim lied in her statement. The first guys to the maroon Merc were Breuning and Carlisle.

> BUD
>
> Dudley's guys. They didn't find the shotguns. They planted them.

*A beat as the magnitude of it all begins to sink in.*

> EXLEY
>
> Somehow it's all connected to Jack's angle. Sid Hudgens. Pictures to blackmail Ellis Loew. A kid got murdered. If we're going to figure this out, we need to work together.

> BUD
>
> Why are you doing this? The Nite Owl made you. You want to tear all that down?

> EXLEY
>
> With a wrecking ball. You want to help me swing it?

*Bud moves to where he stands over Exley. Is he going to kill him or help him?*

> BUD
>
> Let's go see Ellis Loew, find out what the District Attorney knows.

INT. CRIMINAL JUSTICE BLDG. – D.A.'S OUTER
OFFICE – DAY

*A SECRETARY looks up as Bud and Exley beeline Loew's
door.*

> SECRETARY
> You can't go in there!

INT. DISTRICT ATTORNEY'S INNER OFFICE – DAY

*Loew looks up as they burst in.*

> SECRETARY
> Do you want me to call the police, Mr. Loew?

> EXLEY
> Ask for Captain Dudley Smith. Tell him we're
> having a conversation about the death of an
> unemployed actor at a Sunset Strip motel.

*A beat as Loew considers his options.*

> LOEW
> It's okay. These are the police.
>              *(as she leaves)*
> What do you want?

> EXLEY
> I want D.A. Bureau men to tail Dudley Smith

and Pierce Patchett twenty-four hours a day; I
want you to get a judge to authorize wire taps
on their home phones; I want authorization to
check their bank records and I want it all in an
hour.


                        LOEW
On what evidence?


                        BUD
Call it a hunch.


                        LOEW
Absolutely not. Dudley Smith is a highly
decorated member of this city's police
department. I won't smear his and Pierce
Patchett's names without—


                        EXLEY
Without what, them smearing yours first? What
do they have on you, Loew? Pictures of you and
Matt Reynolds with your pants down?


                        LOEW
Do you have any proof?


                        EXLEY
The proof had his throat slit.
                   (a beat)
So far you're not denying it.

> LOEW

I'm not going to dignify this with answers. If
you'll excuse me, I've got a Jack Vincennes
press conference to prepare for.

*Loew enters his bathroom. Bud looks to Exley, who nods:
GO.*

INT. OFFICE BATHROOM – DAY

*Loew is at the mirror clipping a few stray nose hairs.
Bud enters. Exley watches from the b.g.*

> LOEW

Unless you're here to wipe my ass, I believe
we're through.

*Bud moves closer to the sink.*

> LOEW

Don't try this good cop/bad cop crap with me. I
practically invented it. And so what if some
homo actor is dead. Boys, girls, ten of them step
off the bus to L.A. every day.

*Bud slams Loew's face into the mirror, spider-webbing
the glass. Bud swings him around, forces him forward
and shoves his head in the toilet. He holds him there,
finally lets Loew up for breath.*

                        LOEW
    Call him off, Exley!


                        EXLEY
    I don't know how.

*Bud dunks him again, pulls him up.*


                        BUD
    You think you're the A-number-one fucking
    hotshot. Well here's the juice, shitbird. If I take
    you out, there'll be ten more lawyers to take
    your place tomorrow. They just won't come on
    the bus, that's all.

*Bud dunks him again. Holding Loew by the scruff of the
neck, Bud marches him past Exley and back into the . . .*


INT. DISTRICT ATTORNEY'S INNER OFFICE – DAY

*Bud heaves up the window, practically throws Loew
through it. Screaming, Loew catches hold of the window
frame. Bud hammers his hands loose with a fist and
pushes him through.*


EXT. OFFICE WINDOW – DAY

*Bud holds Loew by the legs. Coins, comb and wallet spill
from Loew's pockets, plummet toward the street twelve
floors below.*

LOEW

Okay! Okay! Patchett and Dudley! I wouldn't play ball so they set me up! I gave in. The kid heard everything, so they killed him.

EXLEY

Why? What are Patchett and Dudley up to?

*Bud shakes him some more. Loew's life may depend on the answer.*

                    LOEW
They're taking over Mickey Cohen's rackets.
Because of those pictures I couldn't prosecute!
Oh Jesus, pull me up!


INT. DISTRICT ATTORNEY'S INNER OFFICE – DAY

*Bud hauls Loew back inside, dumps him on the floor. Bruised and bloodied, Loew looks up at Exley as Exley steps up.*


                    EXLEY
Is that how you used to run the good cop/bad
cop?
                    *(to Bud)*
Patchett?

*Bud nods.*


INT. 416 DE MILLE DRIVE (PATCHETT'S) – DAY

*Bud shoulders the heavy door right off its hinges. They enter, guns drawn. Moving quickly, Bud and Exley case the place, working as a team.*


*Double doors on the left open into a library. Ahead, a man sits in a chair, his back to us. Patchett?*

*Bud walks up to him, slowly lowers his gun. Exley steps*

*around. Patchett's arms hang limply at his sides, a pool of blood under each. His wrists have been slit, but even in death there's something elegant about him.*

EXLEY
Looks like his bodyguard had a conflict of
interest.

*Exley spots a typed sheet of paper on a desk.*

*Bud checks Patchett's right hand, the knuckles are split, two of the fingers badly distended.*

> EXLEY
> Suicide note. Says he killed Jack because Jack had figured out a pornography scam Patchett was running.

> BUD
> Slicing himself open wasn't his idea. Two of his fingers are broken.

> EXLEY
> They must have held him there.

> BUD
> Or drugged him.

> EXLEY
> I'd say Dudley's tying up his loose ends. Patchett's dead. He sent you after me.

> BUD
> *(it hits him)*
> Lynn.

*Bud dashes to the phone, dials. It rings. No answer.*

                          BUD

I'll get the car.

*Exley throws him the keys, grabs the phone.*

                          EXLEY

West Hollywood Sheriff. They can be there
before us.


EXT. 1736 ORANGE DRIVE (LYNN BRACKEN'S) –
DAY

*A County Sheriff's unmarked parked out front, a DEP-
UTY standing next to it smoking. Exley's Ford pulls up
behind. As Bud jumps out:*

                          DEPUTY

We took her to the station for safekeeping.
Someone worked her over pretty good. She
wouldn't say who.

*Exley looks at Bud. Bud looks down in shame.*

                          EXLEY

Hold her as Joan Smith. No one sees her unless
I okay it.

                          DEPUTY

All right, Exley.

*As the Deputy moves off:*

                    EXLEY
We should talk to Lynn.

*Bud looks away, shakes his head no. Finally . . .*

                    BUD
You do it.

                    EXLEY
What are you going to do?

                    BUD
I'm going to pay a visit to Sid Hudgens.
Compliment him on his performance at the
Victory Motel.

                    EXLEY
Remember, Bud, we need evidence.

                    BUD
I'll get the evidence.


INT. WEST HOLLYWOOD SHERIFF STATION –
TWILIGHT

*Lynn looks up as Exley enters. Her face is puffy, swollen.*

                    EXLEY
Are you okay?

*She nods, smiles at his bruises.*

LYNN

You okay?

*Exley pulls over a chair, sits opposite her.*

EXLEY
Bud hates himself for what he did.

> LYNN
> *(a beat)*
> I know how he feels.


> EXLEY
> Lynn, I need to know what you can give me on
> Dudley Smith.

*A blank look from her.*


> EXLEY
> He's a police captain. In business with Pierce
> Patchett.


> LYNN
> *(shakes her head)*
> I never heard of him.

*A beat as Exley considers where to go.*


> EXLEY
> Do you have some place you can stay?


> LYNN
> I'll be okay.


EXT. *HUSH-HUSH* MAGAZINE OFFICE (SUNSET
BLVD.) – NIGHT

*Bud arrives to a homicide cordon, crowds of onlookers*

*and press. Hurrying forward, he flashes his badge, en-
ters.*


INT. *HUSH-HUSH* MAGAZINE OFFICE – NIGHT

*A POLICE PHOTOGRAPHER snaps a shot of Hudgens,
who lies broken on the floor by his desk. The office is in
shambles. Bud stops a PASSING DETECTIVE.*


                    BUD
What happened?


                PASSING DETECTIVE
Somebody beat him to death, then stole a bunch
of files. Must've dug up garbage on the wrong
guy.

*The Detective gestures to the page ones tacked to the
wall. Each representing a ruined career.*


                PASSING DETECTIVE
I got it narrowed down to a thousand suspects.

*As Bud thinks, a ROOKIE-TYPE approaches.*


                  ROOKIE-TYPE
Uh—Sergeant White?


                    BUD
*What?*

> ROOKIE-TYPE
>
> Dispatch just got a call for you. Lieutenant
> Exley wants you to meet him at the Victory
> Motel.

EXT. VICTORY MOTEL – NIGHT

*Bud's Packard crests the rise looking down on the Victory. Exley's Ford is in the courtyard; he's leaning against the fender. Bud pulls in, gets out.*

> BUD
>
> You wanted to meet here?

> EXLEY
>
> Me? You called it. I figured Sid Hudgens was . . .

> BUD
> *(interrupting)*
>
> Hudgens is dead.

*As the reality sinks in, Bud and Exley hear tires on the gravel; cars are coming. Being in a concavity, they can't see them yet. The sound of cars stopping on both sides of them.*

> EXLEY
>
> Let's get out of here.

*They hear the clicks of car doors opening. They don't hear them shut.*

> BUD

It's too late.

*Bud steps to his car, grabs a shotgun, some ammunition. Another car pulls up somewhere behind.*

*Resigned, Bud and Exley retreat back. There's movement in the shadows to the left. To the right. They go into room 6.*

INT. VICTORY MOTEL – ROOM 6 – NIGHT

*Adjoining room 5. Really the same space but for a row of bare studs which cuts the room in half. There's a big side window. Bud covers it with a ratty mattress. Exley drops an end table on the counter, blocking the kitchenette window.*

> EXLEY

You figured this was a setup? And you showed up anyway?

*Bud pumps the shotgun. He pulls a .45 automatic and a clip from his waistband.*

> BUD

A lot of bad stuff happened here. It's as good a place as any for it to end. Here.

*He throws the auto and the clip to Exley, pulls out a .38. Bud's armed for bear. They wait in silence. Then:*

EXLEY
You know, all I ever wanted was to measure up to my father.

BUD
Now's your chance. He died in the line of duty, didn't he?

*Gallows humor. Exley looks at him, holds back a laugh. Bud smiles. In another life, they could have been buddies.*

*A creak outside the rear window of room 6. Exley wheels, fires at a shape in the window. The figure of a MAN sprawls back in the dirt.*

*At that, a barrage of gunfire from all sides. Exley and Bud hit the deck as bullets whiz, wood splinters and plaster rains down. Some of the flying debris breaks one of the lenses on Exley's glasses, creases the side of his head.*

*At the first lull, a 2ND MAN shoulders his way hard through the front door of room 5. Bud knocks him back with a blast from the shotgun. In the darkness beyond, muzzle flashes. Exley and Bud duck forward, return fire.*

*Exley empties the .45; Bud does the same with the shot-gun. As they reload . . .*

*The back window breaks behind the mattress, muffled under the gunfire. Bud and Exley look at each other, slide back. Standing to either side, they yank down the mattress and fire simultaneously, tearing TWO MEN apart.*

*Bud and Exley drop to the floor. Whistles and the sound*

*of men advancing. Bud gestures toward the hole in the floor where the hot seat used to be. Exley nods.*

## INT. ROOM 5

*Bud steps between the studs into room 5. He rips back the broken floorboards, drops down out of sight.*

*Exley waits, listens.*

## INT. CRAWLSPACE – NIGHT

*Bud, on his back below the joists. Here and there, a 2 × 4 support rests on a concrete footing. Bud looks around, checking out the chicken wire vents in the siding. TWO SETS OF FEET slide past a vent. Bud rolls to get a bead, fires the shotgun as the feet pass a second vent. Shrieks as the men go down.*

## INT. VICTORY MOTEL – ROOM 6 – NIGHT

*Placing the screams, Exley rushes to the kitchenette, jerks back the end table, jumps up, breaks the glass, and looks out.*

## EXT. VICTORY MOTEL (BEHIND ROOM 6) – NIGHT

*The 5TH and 6TH MEN on the ground. As they try to*

*draw a bead, the last three rounds from Exley's .45 and one from his .38 finish them off.*

INT. VICTORY MOTEL – ROOM 6 – NIGHT

*A 7TH MAN fires from the doorway. Shot through the left shoulder, Exley goes down, twisting and firing back with the .38. The 7th Man falls.*

*A rattle of fire rips in from the door of room 5. Exley fires back a round, clicks on empties. He scuttles back, struggles to reload the .38 . . .*

*The 8TH and 9TH (Breuning) MEN advance. Exley's not going to have time. The 8th Man hears something, notices the hole in the floor. From the darkness below, a shotgun erupts, blasting him back. Breuning reacts, turns. Bud explodes out of the hole. His shotgun thunders once, then twice, and Breuning goes down.*

*Reloading, Bud scrambles to a window, surveys the perimeter. All is quiet.*

> BUD

You okay?

> EXLEY

Yeah.

*Bud goes over to him, reaches down.*

                    BUD

Easy . . .

*He gently pulls Exley to his feet. As Bud's eyes follow Exley up, they widen at something beyond:* Dudley stands in the doorway . . . .38 raised. *He's got nothing to shoot at but Exley's back.*


                    BUD

Move!

*Bud shoves Exley hard to the ground as Dudley fires.*

*The shot passes through Bud's left biceps. Bud drops the shotgun, but goes for Dudley. A second shot rips Bud's chest, but still he comes, trying to draw his pistol. Dudley fires into his chest. Bud falls to the floor and is still.*

*Dudley turns, aims at Exley. A frozen moment as Exley looks up at the senior officer. Exley's expression is strange, and when the words come, they are even stranger.*


                  EXLEY

Rollo Tomasi.

*Dudley reacts.*


                  DUDLEY

Who is he?

                              EXLEY
          You are. You're the guy who gets away with it.
          Jack knew it and so do I.

*The sound of distant POLICE SIRENS. Bud stirs.*

*Dudley cocks back the hammer of the .38. It's over. But
Dudley screams as Bud buries his switchblade into Dud-
ley's left calf. Dudley spins and fires a round down into
Bud's face.*

*Exley goes for Bud's shotgun. Dudley turns, but finds
himself covered by the shotgun. The sirens are getting
closer. Dudley drops the .38.*


                             DUDLEY
          Are you going to shoot me or arrest me?

*Exley doesn't answer, but his eyes betray him.*


                             DUDLEY
          Good. Always the politician. Let me do the
          talking. By the time I'm done, they'll make you
          Chief of Detectives.

*Dudley turns and hobbles out the door.*


EXT. VICTORY MOTEL – NIGHT

*Dudley moves into the motorcourt. Exley steps out of*

*room 5, shotgun still in hand. He looks to the glow of approaching headlights about to crest the hill.*

> DUDLEY
> Hold up your badge so they'll know you're a policeman.

*Dudley raises his badge high over his head. Suddenly,*

*Exley's shotgun belches flame. Dudley goes down, shot in the back. Exley's answer is finally yes.*

*The police cars come over the hill, their headlights illuminating Dudley's body with Exley standing over him. Exley drops the shotgun.*

*As he holds his own badge above his head . . .*

DISSOLVE TO:

INT. CITY HALL DET. BUREAU – OBSERVATION
ROOM – NIGHT

*A midnight assembly. The Chief, D.A. Loew and several high-ranking BRASS. Their attention riveted through the one-way glass into . . .*

INT. INTERROGATION ROOM #1 – NIGHT

*Exhausted, bloody arm bandaged and in a sling, Exley sits across from two INTERNAL AFFAIRS DETECTIVES.*

INTERNAL AFFAIRS ONE
You think you can talk your way out of this,
Lieutenant?

EXLEY
No. But I think I can tell you the truth.

*(he begins)*
During our investigation of events surrounding
the Nite Owl case, Jack Vincennes, Bud White
and I learned the following:

INT. OBSERVATION ROOM – NIGHT

*The Brass watch Exley through the glass, his voice heard
over the speakers.*

LOEW
*(to The Chief)*
Your golden boy's throwing his whole life away.

INT. INTERROGATION ROOM #1 – NIGHT

EXLEY
The three Nite Owl suspects, while guilty of
kidnapping and rape, were innocent of the
multiple homicides at the Nite Owl. The actual
gunmen were most likely Los Angeles Police
Department officers Michael Breuning and
William Carlisle and a third man who may or
may not have been Captain Dudley Smith.

INT. OBSERVATION ROOM – NIGHT

*The Chief and Loew exchange looks of discomfort, dis-*

*tress, then look back at Exley as he continues on the other side of the glass.*

#### EXLEY
*(over speaker)*

Regardless, the crime was committed under the direction of Captain Smith. The objective: the elimination of another police officer, Richard Stensland, who, along with former LAPD officer Leland "Buzz" Meeks, also committed multiple homicides on behalf of Captain Smith and then betrayed him over 25 pounds of heroin, the retrieval of which was the ultimate motivation behind the Nite Owl killings.

INT. INTERROGATION ROOM #1 – NIGHT

*Exley's purging himself; he's finally stopped playing the angles.*

#### EXLEY

Beginning with the incarceration of Mickey Cohen, Captain Smith has been assuming control of organized crime in the city of Los Angeles. This includes the assassination of an unknown number of Mickey Cohen lieutenants, the systematic blackmail of city officials and the murders of Susan Lefferts, Pierce Patchett, Sid Hudgens and Sergeant Jack Vincennes.

Captain Smith admitted as much to me before I shot him at the Victory Motel. That's it.

*He takes a deep breath.*


INT. OBSERVATION ROOM – NIGHT

*Loew, The Chief and the Brass confer as the Internal Affairs Detectives leave Exley alone in the interrogation room.*

> LOEW
> The press will have a field day with this.


> BRASS #1
> It'll stain the department for years.


> THE CHIEF
> Decades.


> LOEW
> If we could convince the kid to play ball, who's to say how Dudley Smith died?


INT. INTERROGATION ROOM #1 – NIGHT

*Exley, all alone in the quiet room, catches sight of himself in the mirrored window. He meets his own gaze, holds it a beat, then smiles. He can't see him, but he is*

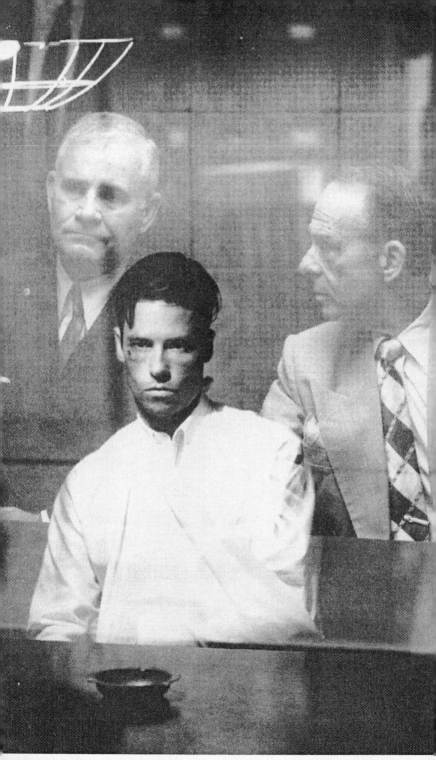

*looking right at The Chief. Suddenly, the speaker over-
head crackles to life.*

> THE CHIEF'S VOICE
> You want to tell me what you're smiling about?

> EXLEY
> A hero.

INT. OBSERVATION ROOM – NIGHT

*The men look at each other. How did he know?*

> THE CHIEF
> And?

*Exley stares back at faces he can't see. He plays the
angle.*

> EXLEY
> *(over speaker)*
> In this situation, you're going to need more
> than one.

*D.A. Loew looks at The Chief. The Chief considers a beat,
then . . .*

CUT TO:

*LOS ANGELES EXAMINER* HEADLINE:

*LAPD BATTLES ORGANIZED CRIME*
*AT ABANDONED MOTEL*
*Hero's Death for Famed Police Captain*

INT. CITY HALL ROTUNDA – DAY

*Exley in his dress blues, his left arm in a white sling. Flashbulbs pop as The Chief pins a medal on his chest. The Chief steps to a microphone.*

> THE CHIEF
> Next year the LAPD will move into its new
> facility. With leaders like two-time Medal of
> Valor recipient Detective Lieutenant Edmund
> Exley, the image of fat cops stealing apples will
> be left behind forever and Los Angeles will
> finally have the police force it deserves.

*Applause. More flashbulbs. Exley spots someone: Lynn, watching from all the way in the back. Her once flowing hair is cut short. Looks even better. Exley goes over.*

> EXLEY
> *(ironic smile)*
> I tried to throw it all away and they gave it back
> in spades.

*Lynn smiles. She knows better.*

                    LYNN
You couldn't resist.

*Exley can't help but smile. She's got his number.*

                    EXLEY
They're using me and for a little while I'm using
them.

*They walk away together. She takes his arm.*


EXT. CITY HALL – DAY

*Bud sits in the back of a parked car. Braces on his legs,
head sutured. Jaw wired shut and tubes running in and
out. Exley bends down at the window. Bud forces a
smile through the wires, tries to say something, but
can't. Exley can, but doesn't know where to start. Finally:*


                    EXLEY
Thanks for the push.

*Bud raises his hand. Exley takes it. Although Bud can't
speak, he says it all with a nod.*


                    EXLEY
Yeah.

*A final nod, and Exley steps back. He looks to Lynn. A*

*departing well-wisher calls out a congratulation to Exley.*

> LYNN
> Some men get the world. Others get ex-hookers
> and a trip to Arizona.

*A beat. Maybe Exley wishes he'd gotten the trip to Arizona. She kisses him on the cheek.*

*Lynn gets in the car. Starts it. Exley looks back at Bud. The car moves. A turn into traffic, a goodbye wave from Bud. Exley's all alone. As he watches them go . . .*

FADE TO BLACK.

*THE END*

# Cast

| | |
|---|---|
| Bud White | RUSSELL CROWE |
| Ed Exley | GUY PEARCE |
| Jack Vincennes | KEVIN SPACEY |
| Dudley Smith | JAMES CROMWELL |
| Lynn Bracken | KIM BASINGER |
| Sid Hudgens | DANNY DeVITO |
| Pierce Patchett | DAVID STRATHAIRN |
| D.A. Ellis Loew | RON RIFKIN |
| | |
| *Badge of Honor* Star | |
|   Brett Chase | MATT MCCOY |
| Mickey Cohen | PAUL GUILFOYLE |
| Johnny Stompanato | PAOLO SEGANTI |
| Dick Stensland | GRAHAM BECKEL |
| Jack's Dancing Partner | SYMBA SMITH |
| Liquor Store Owner | WILL ZAHRN |
| Susan Lefferts | AMBER SMITH |
| Buzz Meeks | DARRELL SANDEEN |
| Matt Reynolds | SIMON BAKER DENNY |
| Tammy Jordan | SHAWNEE FREE JONES |
| Police Chief | JOHN MAHON |
| Dudley's Guys: | |
|   Breuning | TOMAS ARANA |
|   Carlisle | MICHAEL MCCLEERY |
| Vice Captain | JACK CONLEY |
| Forensic Chief | GENE WOLANDE |
| Coroner | MICHAEL CHIEFFO |
| Mrs. Lefferts | GWENDA DEACON |
| City Councilman | JIM METZLER |
| Boxer | ROBERT BARRY FLEMING |
| Nite Owl Suspects: | |
|   Ray Collins | JEREMIAH BIRKETT |
|   Louis Fontaine | SALIM GRANT |
|   Ty Jones | KARREEM WASHINGTON |
| Inez Soto | MARISOL PADILLA SANCHEZ |
| Lana Turner | BRENDA BAKKE |

# L.A. Confidential

## ORIGINAL SOUNDTRACK AVAILABLE ON RESTLESS RECORDS

### FEATURING

CHET BAKER

MILES DAVIS

JACKIE GLEASON

BETTY HUTTON

DEAN MARTIN

JOHNNY MERCER

GERRY MULLIGAN

KAY STARR

LEE WILEY

JERRY GOLDSMITH

www.restless.com